HISTORICAL ROMANCES
MAKE FALLING IN LOVE
SIMPLE AND SWEET

WANDA E. BRUNSTETTER

ISBN 978-1-61626-455-0

All scripture quotations are taken from the King James Version of the Bible.

This book is a work of fiction. Names, characters, places, and incidents are either products of the author's imagination or used fictitiously. Any similarity to actual people, organizations, and/or events is purely coincidental.

For more information about Wanda E. Brunstetter, please access the author's website at the following Internet address:
www.wandabrunstetter.com

Cover design: Faceout Studio, www.faceoutstudio.com
Cover photography: Steve Gardner, Pixelworks Studios

Published by Barbour Publishing, Inc., P.O. Box 719, Uhrichsville, OH 44683, www.barbourbooks.com

Our mission is to publish and distribute inspirational products offering exceptional value and biblical encouragement to the masses.

Printed in the United States of America.

CONTENTS

DADDY'S GIRL

DEDICATION

To my husband, Richard. . .
Thanks for your interest in history.
I appreciate your love and support.

CHAPTER 1

August 1879

"All aboard!" The conductor's booming cry pulled Glenna Moore to her feet. She glanced down at her father, slouched on the wooden bench outside the train station in Central City, Nebraska. His head was supported only by the unyielding plank wall, and his mouth hung slightly open.

Glenna bent down and gave his shoulder a good shake. "Wake up, Daddy. The train's here, and we've got to go now."

Her father groaned and swiped one hand across his unruly goatee. "Leave me alone, girl. I wanna sleep."

Glenna dropped back onto the bench with a heavy sigh, making no effort to conceal her disgust. "You can sleep all you want once we're on the train." She poked him in the ribs with a bony elbow. "You don't want to be thrown in jail, do you?"

Glenna's harsh reminder of their dire circumstances seemed to be enough motivation for Daddy. He opened one eye, then the other, yawning widely as he attempted to stand up. His equilibrium was not what it should have been, however, and he was forced to grab hold of Glenna's arm in order to keep from falling over.

Allowing Daddy to lean on her small frame, Glenna complained, "If you just hadn't been so determined to finish that bottle of whiskey, you might not be in such a state right now!"

The empty bottle was lying on the floor by their bench, and she sneered at it as though it were her worst enemy.

"Needed it," her father mumbled. "Was dealt a raw hand."

No, Daddy, Glenna lamented silently, *it was you who dealt the bad hand.* Ever since Mama died in childbirth, along with her little brother, Glenna had been Daddy's girl. She needed him as much as he needed her, so she would make every effort to bridle her tongue where his problem was concerned.

"If we don't get on board that train heading west, it's going to leave without us." Glenna shuddered. "And if we stay here, the law will either put you in jail or some sidewinder's bound to shoot you."

Her father snorted and gave the empty whiskey bottle a hefty kick with the toe of his sable-colored boot. "Humph! Can I help it if I'm better at poker than most of those snakes in the grass?"

In all her eighteen years, Glenna could never remember her daddy admitting he was wrong about anything—not even cheating at the card tables. She was well aware of Daddy's special vest, with a single strip of elastic sewn inside. She'd seen those marked cards he kept hidden there, too. Glenna had no right to complain or judge her father though. After all, he protected her and took care of her needs. Well, most of them anyway.

Glenna glanced down at her dark-green, cotton day dress with its formfitting bodice and tight, short sleeves. The lower part of the gown consisted of both an underskirt and an overskirt, pulled slightly up in the back, giving it a somewhat bustled look. While it had cost a tidy sum when she'd purchased it a few years back, it was now quite out-of-date. Daddy hadn't done too well at his trade recently, and new dresses weren't a priority—at least not to his way of thinking.

Smoke and cinders belched from the diamond-shaped stack on top of the Union Pacific's mighty engine. The imperious screech of the locomotive whistle and another "All aboard!" drove Glenna's troubled thoughts to the back of her mind. "We've got to board that train, Daddy."

Her father bent down and grabbed his well-worn suitcase, and Glenna followed suit. Due to their rapid departure, they were traveling light. Since they had no additional luggage, there wasn't a need for anything to be placed in the baggage car.

Gripping Daddy's arm, Glenna guided him toward the conductor.

"Tickets, please!" the gray-haired gentleman barked, thrusting out his hand.

Glenna set her suitcase down and fumbled in her handbag. She retrieved the tickets and handed them to the conductor, just in time to grab her father's arm before he toppled over.

"Too bad you're not in a private Pullman car," the conductor said with a sympathetic look. "Granger, Wyoming, is a ways off. It appears as though your traveling companion could do with a bit of privacy."

Glenna gritted her teeth and offered the man a curt nod as he helped her board the train. No one wished more for a private car than she. Funds were low just now, and spending what little they did have on something so unnecessary was not a good idea. Until they got settled in the town of Granger, their money must be spent wisely. That meant riding in a dismal, overcrowded emigrants' coach for third-class passengers who soon would become a congregation of aching spines and flaring tempers.

Visions of more affluent times flashed into Glenna's mind. Just thinking about their present situation sent a chord of defiance through her soul. She hoped things wouldn't always be like this. Daddy kept assuring her that someday he would hit it really big. Then he'd build a house they could call their own, buy lots of fancy clothes, and give Glenna a horse and buggy fit for a princess. It would probably never happen, but dreaming of better days was all that kept her going.

Her father had already stumbled up the steps and was slouched against one wall when Glenna joined him moments later. "We must find a bench," she said in a voice laced with frustration. If Daddy kept standing there like a disfigured statue, they'd not only have trouble securing a seat, but they would probably be the laughingstock of the entire coach!

With another one of his pathetic groans, Daddy pulled away from the wall. Grabbing Glenna's free arm, he began shuffling down the aisle.

Glenna felt, rather than saw, the curious stares from the other passengers as they awkwardly made their way toward a vacant wooden bench. She kept her eyes focused on her goal so she wouldn't have to view the pity or disgust from those nearby. Why couldn't Daddy have stayed sober today? Why must *she* suffer the humiliation of his actions?

She drew in a deep breath, then blew it out with such force she felt the tiny curls across her forehead bounce. As far back as she could remember, things had been this way where Daddy was concerned. She hated to admit it, but barring some unforeseen miracle, she knew things would probably never be any different.

Daddy dropped his suitcase and gave it a good kick under their seat. Then he flopped onto the hard bench. Glenna placed her own piece of luggage next to his and slid in beside him, thankful they would no longer be viewed by the entire car. Maybe now she could find a few moments of peace.

David Green pulled methodically on the end of his recently trimmed beard as he studied the young woman in the seat directly across the aisle. Dark ringlets framed her oval face, and her high-necked dress, though slightly outdated, fit just right. He couldn't help but notice her flushed cheeks, wary expression, and the obvious tension in her body. She probably had her hands full with that man who sat beside her. Was the drunkard her father, perhaps an uncle, or even a much too old husband?

David shook his head. Surely this delicate beauty could not be married to such an uncouth fellow! Those long, ebony curls and fetching brown eyes could easily have wooed a younger, more distinguished, and pleasant man than the one sitting next to her. Why, the paunchy, middle-aged man was slouched in his seat as though he hadn't a care in the world.

How despicable. Then a verse of scripture popped into David's mind. *"Judge not, that ye be not judged."* He swallowed hard. *Thank You for reminding me, Lord. But for the grace of God, there go I.*

David's thoughts were pulled aside as the man who shared his seat spoke up. He blinked. "What was that?"

"I said, 'When do you think the train will pull out?' " the young man asked. "We've already had several delays today, and I'm getting anxious to see this trip come to an end."

David turned his full attention to his chum—a name given to those who shared seats on the emigrants' coach. The man was already onboard the train when David got on in Omaha, Nebraska. He'd introduced himself as Alexander P. Gordon, a Scottish author and poet. He boasted of having a modest reputation as a "travel writer."

Before David could open his mouth to reply to Alexander's question, the train whistle blew three quick blasts, and their humble coach began to rock from side to side. The swaying motion was almost gentle and lulling at first, but as the train picked up speed, David could hear the familiar *clickety-clack, slap-slap-slap* of the wheels. Soon their car began to bounce like a rolling ship at sea.

David tried to ignore the distraction and smiled at his companion. "Guess that answers your question about when we'll be leaving Central City."

Alexander nodded. "Yes, indeed."

A boisterous hiccup from across the aisle pulled David's attention back to the lovely young woman and the inebriated man whose head was now leaning on her slender shoulder. She looked so melancholy—almost hopeless, in fact. His heart went out to her, and he wondered what he might do or say to make her feel better. After all, it was his calling to minister to others.

"Tell me about this place where you have been called to serve, Reverend Green."

David turned back toward Alexander, but the man's attention seemed to be more focused on his red, irritated wrists, which he kept scratching, than on what he'd just said to David. Alexander had told him earlier that he'd acquired a rather pustulant itch. Probably from the cramped quarters aboard the train he'd ridden before meeting up with David.

"I'll be shepherding my first flock in a mining town known as Idaho City," David replied, averting his gaze from Alexander's raw, festering wrists back to the woman across the aisle.

"Hmm. . .that would be in Idaho Territory, if I'm not mistaken."

David nodded. "Quite right."

"And you said you recently left divinity school?"

"Actually, it was Hope Academy in Omaha. I just finished my training a few weeks ago."

"Ah, so you are what some Americans refer to as a 'greenhorn'?"

David chuckled. "Some might say so. However, I have had some experience preaching. In fact, I spent a few years as a circuit rider before I decided to attend the academy and further my ministerial studies."

"I see. So, are you married or single?"

David's eyebrows shot up. "I'm single. Why do you ask?"

Alexander frowned. "Most men of the cloth are married, aren't they? I would think it might even be a requirement."

"Why's that?"

"Too many temptations. The world is full of carnal women who would like nothing better than to drag a religious man straight to the ground."

David chewed on his lower lip as he pondered this thought. Perhaps Mr. Gordon was right. It could be that he'd been too hasty in accepting this call from the good people of Idaho City Community Church. He thought about the letter inside his coat pocket. It was from one of the church deacons, and as he recalled, it made some reference to him being married. In fact, the deacon's exact words had been: "The ladies here are anxious to meet your wife. I'm sure she will feel quite welcome in our church and soon become a part of our growing community as well."

I wonder what could have given them the idea that I'm married, David reflected. *Perhaps Alexander is right. It could be an expected thing for the shepherd of a church to have a wife.*

A deep rumbling, followed by a high-pitched whine, drew David's attention back to the young lady across from him. The man's loud snoring was clearly distressing to the woman, and she squirmed restlessly in her seat.

If only my chum would keep quiet a few moments, I might think of something appropriate to say to her.

Though more than a bit irritated, David listened patiently as Alexander began a narration of the many illnesses which had plagued him all of his twenty-nine years. David was twenty-six, and he hadn't had half as many ailments as this poor chap.

As though by divine intervention, Alexander suddenly became quiet. David cast a quick glance in his direction and found that his chum had drifted off to sleep. Drawing in a deep breath and sending up a quick prayer, David made a hasty decision. He would get out of his seat, walk across the aisle, and see if that young lady was in need of his counsel.

CHAPTER 2

Two men dressed in dark suits sat in the seat directly across from Glenna. One seemed intent on scratching his wrists while the other man kept staring at her. At least she thought he was looking her way. Maybe he was just watching the scenery out her window. *But why wouldn't he watch out the window nearest him?* she wondered. *Surely there's nothing on my side of the tracks which would hold any more appeal than what he can see over there.*

Glenna swallowed hard as she glanced across the aisle again. This time she studied the man's features. They were strong and clean—a straight nose, dark-brown hair, parted on the side and cut just below the ears, and a matching well-trimmed beard. She couldn't be sure of the exact color of his eyes from this distance, but they appeared to be either green or perhaps a soft gray. They weren't dark like hers, of that much she was certain.

Her heart did a little flip-flop when he nodded slightly and offered her a pleasant smile. He was easily the most handsome man she'd ever seen. She returned his smile with a tentative one of her own.

Daddy was snoring loudly now, and she elbowed him in the ribs, hoping to halt the irritating buzz. How would she ever catch the eye of an attractive man if her father kept making such a spectacle of himself? If Daddy appeared disagreeable, then so did she. At least, that's the way Glenna perceived it. If only she had a jar of canned tomatoes to cure the hangover he would undoubtedly have.

Her mind wandered back in time as she remembered how they'd been staying at Prudence Montgomery's Boardinghouse in Sioux City, Iowa. Daddy had come back to their room late one night. He'd been "working" and had guzzled a few too many glasses of whiskey.

Glenna shuddered as she thought about the scene he'd made, yelling and cursing at poor Prudence for not keeping his supper warm. When he'd finally ambled off to bed, Prudence had turned on Glenna. "Gambling is evil—spawned by the devil himself." She sniffed deeply and lifted her chin. "If you don't watch yourself, young lady, you'll grow up to be just like your drunken daddy. Like father, like daughter, that's what I have to say!"

Maybe it's true, Glenna thought ruefully. *Maybe I'll never be anything more than a gambler's daughter.*

"Excuse me, miss, but I was wondering if you might like to borrow a pillow."

A melodic, deep voice drew Glenna back to the present, and the distinct fragrance of bay rum cologne tickled her nose. She jerked her head and looked up at a pleasant face with a pair of soft-green eyes. Her heart jumped into her throat when he sent her a melting glance.

"A pillow?" she squeaked.

"For your companion."

Glenna swiveled back toward her sleeping father, whose head drooped heavily against her shoulder. Daddy would probably be more comfortable with a pillow, and so would she. Should she accept anything from a complete stranger though? Despite his present condition, Daddy was well learned, and among other things, he'd taught her to be wary of outsiders—especially men.

As if the young man could read her mind, he extended a hand. "I'm Reverend David Green." He motioned toward his seat companion. "Between the two of us, my sleeping chum and I possess three straw-filled pillows, so we can certainly spare one."

Glenna shook the offered hand, though somewhat hesitantly. Even if he was a man of the cloth, she was still a bit uncertain about speaking to Reverend Green. "My name's Glenna Moore, and this is my father, Garret." She tilted her head in Daddy's direction. His mouth was hanging slightly open, and she felt the heat of embarrassment creep up the back of her neck, then spread quickly to her face.

"It's nice to meet you, Glenna. May I use your given name?"

She smiled shyly and nodded. "Yes, Reverend Green."

"Then please be so kind as to call me David."

Glenna had only met a few ministers, and those had all been "fire-and-brimstone" parsons who stood on the street corners shouting out warnings of doom and gloom. As she looked into David's kind eyes, she decided there would be nothing wrong with calling him by his first name. After all, he had asked her to, and what could it possibly hurt?

She lifted her chin and smiled. "David, then."

David's throat constricted, and he drew in a deep, unsteady breath. He hoped Glenna didn't realize how nervous he was. He'd met lots of attractive women in his life, but none had held the appeal this young woman did. He'd noticed how breathtakingly beautiful she was from the moment she had boarded the train. Was it her long, curly, dark hair or those penetrating mahogany eyes? Maybe it was her soft, full lips that made his palms begin to sweat. Perhaps it was her forlorn expression that drew him like a moth charging toward a dancing fire. He imagined how she might feel held securely in his arms. What would it be like to bury his face in her deep-brown hair? How would her ivory skin feel beneath his fingers?

David shook his head, trying to clear away such errant thoughts. He shouldn't be thinking this way. What had come over him all of a sudden? Maybe he was merely in need of more pleasant company than Alexander—the poet with itchy wrists, stories about ill health, and tales of lengthy journeys.

The train made a sudden, unexpected lurch, and David grasped the back of Glenna's seat to steady himself. His ears burned at the thought of being pitched into her lap. As it was, the disconcerting jolt had brought his face mere inches from hers.

Garret Moore's eyes popped open before David had a chance to right himself and gain his composure. "I say there," the man sputtered. "And who might you be?"

"Daddy, this is Reverend David Green," Glenna answered, before David could even open his mouth. "He's seated across the aisle."

David extended one hand, while hanging onto the seat back with the other. "Nice to meet you, sir."

Garret wrinkled his bulbous, crimson nose and made no effort to shake hands. "What's your business, son?"

"I–I'm a minister of the Gospel."

"Not your profession, you idiot!" Garret bellowed. "What business do you have with my daughter?"

Taken aback, David began to stutter—something he hadn't done since he was a young boy. "I—I—w–was—just—"

Obviously aware of his distress, Glenna came quickly to the rescue. "David was kind enough to offer me one of his pillows, Daddy."

One dark eyebrow shot up as Garret tipped his head, apparently sizing David up. "Is that so?"

David nodded. "The pillow was actually for you, sir. I

thought it might be more comfortable than your daughter's shoulder." Feeling a bit more sure of himself now, he smiled. At least he was no longer stuttering like an addle-brained child.

"Just what do you know about Glenna's shoulder?" Garret shouted at the top of his lungs.

David dipped his head. "N–nothing at all."

Glenna's father squinted his glassy-blue eyes and waved a husky hand toward David. "We're not some kind of charity case, you know. If either Glenna or I have need of a sleeping board or pillow, I'll hail the news butcher and purchase one."

Glenna offered David an apologetic smile. "Thank you for the kind offer, but we'll manage just fine."

David felt sure this was her way of asking him to return to his seat. From the irritated look on her father's face, he was also quite certain the unpleasant man would probably create a nasty scene if he didn't leave soon. He nodded slightly, looking only at Glenna. "If you need anything, you know where to find me."

She smiled. "Thank you. I'll remember that."

David shuffled back to his seat, feeling much like a whipped pup coming home with its tail between its legs. Groveling went against his nature, yet he knew it would be wrong to create a scene. *You're a new man in Christ now,* a small voice whispered. *Let Me fight your battles.*

Glenna glanced at her father, hoping he wouldn't say anything about her making conversation with a complete stranger.

Surely he must realize that David, being a man of God and all, wouldn't cause me any harm.

Daddy gave her a grim frown, followed by a raucous yawn. "I can't believe you, Glenna. I lay my head down to take a little catnap, and what do you go and do behind my back?" Before she could reply, he continued his tirade. "You started getting all cozylike with some man, that's what you did. And a black-suited, Bible-thumpin' preacher at that!" He shook one finger in her face. "What's gotten into you, girl? Have you no more brains than a turnip?"

Glenna cringed. Daddy's deep voice had raised at least an octave, and the last thing she wanted was for David Green to overhear this ridiculous tongue-lashing.

"I wasn't getting cozy with the preacher," she defended. "I was merely being polite after he so kindly offered us one of his pillows."

"Humph! That man has designs on you," her father snapped. "I know the look of a man on the prowl. Why, I oughta speak with the conductor and have the cad thrown off this train!"

Glenna grabbed her father's coat sleeve. "Please, don't. David. . .I mean, Reverend Green has taken his seat. I'm sure he won't bother us again."

Her father gave the end of his scraggly goatee a few sharp pulls, then he shrugged. "I'll let it go for now, but if that scoundrel bothers you again, I'm going to report him immediately. Is that clear?"

Glenna nodded solemnly. She knew Daddy meant what he said. He was not a man given to idle threats. If he said he would do something, he most certainly would. She scowled. *Of course, that doesn't include winning big. Sometimes, when the cards are in his favor, he makes a real killing. Other times, like last night, Daddy gets caught cheating, and then . . .*

Glenna clamped her teeth tightly together. She wouldn't dwell on last night's happenings. Daddy had been cornered by those professional gamblers, threatened with his life, then run out of town. Their brief time in Central City, Nebraska, had come to an end, and that was that. It wasn't the first time something like this had happened, and it probably wouldn't be the last. Glenna knew she should learn to accept things as they were and quit wishing for a miracle which would probably never happen. She closed her eyes and tried to relax. She wouldn't think about that good-looking man across the aisle, and she wouldn't keep hoping for Daddy to change!

CHAPTER 3

David had just closed his eyes and was about to doze off when his chum spoke up.

"Would you like to hear one of my poems?"

The last thing on David's mind was poetry, but he nodded agreeably. "Sure, why not?"

Whipping a crumpled piece of paper from his coat pocket, Alexander opened it with a flourish. There was obvious pride on his face as he began reading. When he finished, the poet turned to face David, a questioning look in his eyes.

Never having cared much for poetic rhyme, David offered a forced smile. "That was. . .unique." It was the kindest thing he could think of to say.

Alexander's face broke into a smile. "You really think so?"

David nodded, feeling much like a rabbit caught in a trap. "Unique. . .yes, very."

Alexander refolded the piece of paper, this time being careful not to rumple it. David's encouraging words must have bolstered his confidence, for the twinkle in his eyes gave indication that he was a man with a mission. Alexander placed the poem back into his pocket. "I've written an essay, too. It's entitled 'Travels in the Mountains on Foot.' "

David raised his eyebrows. "A rather unusual title, isn't it?"

Alexander nodded. "Perhaps, but it's an account of a journey I made about a year ago. It took me through the mountains in southern France."

I can't imagine this sickly little man making such a trip, David mused. *There must be more to him than meets the eye.*

"The adventures from this train trip will also become an essay," Alexander continued. "I believe I shall call it 'Across the Plains.' "

David smiled. "An appropriate title for now, but once we leave Nebraska, our journey will take us through some rugged mountain ranges."

Alexander frowned. "At least I won't be overtaking it on foot."

"The train is much better transportation," David agreed.

"Even with all its irritating stops and starts. I couldn't believe it when the train was held up for nearly an hour because a silly cow was standing stubbornly on the tracks." Alexander squirmed uneasily. "And these uncomfortable benches are far too short for anyone but a child!"

David chuckled. "You must have a powerful good reason for going all the way to California in an overcrowded, unsanitary emigrants' car."

Alexander's eyes opened wide. "Did I not tell you my mission?"

"I don't believe so." The truth was, ever since Glenna Moore and her disagreeable father had boarded the train, David's thoughts had been detoured. Often while Alexander was talking to him, he'd been watching the lovely young woman across the aisle instead of listening.

He glanced her way again, but she seemed to be engrossed with the passing scenery out her window. Her father, on the other hand, was holding a deck of cards. Every few seconds he would shuffle them with bravado, using his battered suitcase as a kind of table balanced on his knees.

"So, in a few weeks, I hope to be married."

Alexander's last words brought David's attention back into focus. "Married? You're getting married soon?"

"Yes, to Annie Osgood. I just told you, she lives in California and hasn't been well. I'm hoping my presence will bring her around. As soon as she's on the mend, we plan to be wed."

David clamped his mouth shut, afraid he might burst out laughing. A sickly man, traveling all the way to California, on a train he detested, in order to marry a frail woman? What sense did that make?

"I love Annie very much," Alexander said, as though he had some insight as to the questions swirling around in David's muddled brain.

David smiled. "I wish you all the best."

A cloud of black smoke curled past the window as the train moved steadily down the tracks. Glenna leaned close to the glass, studying the passing scenery with interest. Here and there, scattered buildings dotted the land, but mostly there was just prairie. . .miles and miles of dusty earth reaching up to the blistering sun high overhead.

Glenna repositioned herself against the stiff, unyielding wooden bench, cutting into her backside. Feeling the need for a walk, she stood up and stretched her arms over her head, hoping to dislodge a few of the kinks. Maybe a stroll to the front of the narrow, box-shaped car would help. Daddy was engaged in a game of poker with a group of rowdy men near the back of the coach where the water closet was located. She craned her neck and noticed he was engrossed in his work, as usual. He'd never even know she'd left her seat.

Glenna glanced candidly at the two distinguished-looking men who shared the seat across from her. They both appeared to be sleeping. She wished she could speak to Reverend Green again. . .maybe offer some kind of apology for her father's earlier rude behavior. She rotated her shoulders a few times, then started up the aisle. It soon became apparent that she would need to grab the back of each seat as she proceeded up the aisle. She could only hope the train wouldn't jerk suddenly, sending her toppling to the floor. Glenna would be so relieved when the train made its next stop. It was hot enough to pop corn inside this stuffy car! Some fresh air and a chance to walk on solid ground would be a most welcome relief, not to mention an opportunity for a quick bite to eat.

By the time she made it to the front of the coach, Glenna's legs felt like rubber, and rivulets of perspiration ran down her forehead. She stepped through the door and onto the small platform which separated their car from the one ahead. Gulping in the only fresh air available, she steadied herself against the metal railing. In spite of the day's heat, the continual breeze from the moving train seemed cool and inviting.

Glenna licked her dry lips and swallowed hard. Her throat felt parched, and she wished she'd had the good sense to bring along a canteen filled with water. What had she been thinking of? She'd ridden the train before. She knew there were times when endless stretches of uninhabited land meant no stops at all.

She moistened her lips again. At this very moment, she'd have gladly given away what few possessions she owned in order to have something to quench her thirst. To make matters worse, she'd forgotten to pack a linen duster to wear over her traveling dress. She knew how dust could filter through the open windows, sifting, penetrating, and finally pervading everything in sight. No amount of brushing or shaking would ever remove it all either. After a few days on the train, Glenna would probably hate herself, as well as the cursed dust.

"Are you all right, Miss Moore?" A deep, male voice, whose words were spoken loud enough to be heard over the noisy *clickety-clack* of the train's steel wheels, caused Glenna to jump.

David Green stood a few feet away, a look of concern etched on his handsome face.

"I saw you come out here," he explained. "When you tarried, I became concerned."

Glenna's stomach reeled with nervousness. "It's kind of you to worry about me, Reverend Green, but—"

"David. Please, call me David."

"I needed some fresh air, and I'm thirsty as a hound dog." She moistened her lips one more time. "Other than that, I'm perfectly fine."

He chuckled, and there was a distinctive twinkle in his emerald eyes. *He really is a charming man. Why would Daddy object to me speaking with someone as kind as David?*

"Have you anything to drink?"

Glenna shook her head. "Daddy and I were in such a hurry to leave Central City, neither of us thought to fill a canteen." She sighed deeply. "I don't think clearly when I'm under pressure, and Daddy wasn't in any condition to think at all."

David's twinkle was gone now. In its place was obvious compassion. "I have a listening ear, if you'd care to talk about anything."

She swallowed hard and sucked in her lower lip to keep from blurting out her frustrations. This man seemed honest and genuinely concerned for her welfare. Maybe she should swallow her pride and open up to him about some of her troubles. *He might even be able to help somehow. After all, he is a preacher, and men of God are supposed to have words of wisdom to offer, aren't they?*

Glenna was on the verge of telling David why she and Daddy were on this particular train when the door of their coach flew open. Her father, red-faced and sweating profusely, lumbered onto the platform.

"Daddy, what is it? You look upset," Glenna declared. Was he angry with her for coming out here alone? Or were his labored breathing and crimson face due to the rage he felt at seeing her and David together?

With a sense of urgency, Daddy grabbed Glenna's arm. His face was pinched, as though he were in pain. "I love you, Glenna. No matter what happens, please remember that."

Before she could respond, Daddy gave her a quick hug, threw one leg over the metal railing, and plunged off the train.

CHAPTER 4

Glenna let out a scream that echoed in her ears. *"Daddy!"*

She leaned over the iron railing, her eyes scanning the ground below for any sign of her father. The train was moving too fast. She could see nothing but the blur of trees and thick dust swirling through the air. There was no sign of Daddy anywhere. Had he fallen under the train? Was he lying wounded in the dirt somewhere? Was he. . .dead?

David grabbed Glenna by one arm and pulled her away from the railing. She buried her face in his chest and sobbed. "Daddy! Daddy! Oh, why would he jump from the train like that?"

David patted her gently on the back. "I have no idea, but—"

His comforting words were halted when two burly-looking

men came running onto the platform. One of them was dressed in a dark suit with a plaid vest. The other wore a Stetson and a tooled leather belt.

"Where is he? Where is that scum? I oughta lay him out like a side of beef!" the taller man bellowed.

"He came through this door!" the other one shouted. "Now where's he hiding, anyways?"

When she noticed the guns nestled at both men's hips, Glenna's heart began to pound. Unable to answer, she merely swallowed and hung her head.

The shorter man's fingers danced in a nervous gesture over the trigger of his weapon. "I'll bet that low-down snake ran into the next car. He's probably lurkin' behind some poor old lady's skirts, thinkin' she'll save his sorry hide." The man squinted his beady, dark eyes. "I'll blow the hair off anyone's head who's dumb enough to protect the likes of Garret Moore!"

Glenna pulled back from David and thrust her chin out defiantly, but it quivered nonetheless. "You needn't bother looking in the next coach. My father is gone."

"Gone? What do ya mean 'gone'?" the taller man asked.

"He jumped off the train," David explained.

The shorter man peered over the railing, as if he expected to see something more than the passing scenery. "You'd better be tellin' the truth about this."

"Why would we lie about something so awful?" Glenna's voice shook with raw emotion, and she covered her mouth with the palm of her hand.

David reached out to clasp her hand. "Miss Moore is right.

We have no reason to hide anything from you."

The taller man shrugged. "If that simple-minded sidewinder jumped off a train goin' at this speed, then he got his just reward."

Glenna shuddered. This was her father they were talking about. Daddy had more than his share of faults—even cheated at the card tables from time to time—but he was no simple-minded sidewinder!

"You take that back!" she cried, jerking her hand free from David's. She began to buffet the shorter man's chest with her small fists. "My daddy loved me! He'd never have jumped unless he'd been forced into doing such a terrible thing."

"Ha! He was forced, all right!" the big man blustered. "He either had to give our money back or take a bullet in the head."

Glenna trembled, realizing her father's choices had been limited—either die at the hand of another gambler or jump to his death from a moving train. Of course, he could have given the men their money. Better yet, Daddy should have resigned his unsavory lifestyle and gotten a decent, law-abiding job years ago. *He could have given up drinking, too,* she thought bitterly. His addiction to the bottle had only brought them untold grief.

The shorter man snorted. "Guess there ain't no use hangin' out here, Sam. The girl's daddy is gone, and so's our hard-earned cash."

Glenna's heart was thumping with fury now. "Hard-earned?" she shrieked. "If you two make a living the same way my father did, there was nothing *hard-earned* about the money you lost!"

Sam sneered at her. "You're pretty feisty for a little slip of a gal." He moved aggressively toward her. "Why, I oughta—"

David stepped quickly between Glenna and the gambler. "I'm sure the lady meant no disrespect."

Glenna's lower lip began to twitch. "I can speak for myself, thank you very much."

Sam snorted again and turned to face his buddy. "Come on, Rufus. Let's get back to our game. I'm sure we can recoup some of our losses if we find a few more saps to play the next hand." He glared at Glenna. "This little filly ain't worth us wastin' no more time on."

Rufus nodded. Then, brushing past them, his elbow bumped David in the back as he sauntered into the coach. Sam was right on his heels.

David drew in a deep breath. "Whew, that was close."

"Close? What do you mean, 'close'?"

"Those men had guns, Glenna. If your father hadn't jumped off the train, they would have shot him." David looked her straight in the eye. "And if I hadn't stepped in and softened them up a bit, they might have shot you."

Glenna's mouth dropped open like a broken hinge. She'd been so upset about Daddy jumping from the train that she hadn't realized her own life might be in danger. She chewed her bottom lip and winced when she tasted blood. "What does it matter? Without Daddy, I have no life."

David followed Glenna back to their dreary coach, wondering what he might say or do to help ease her pain. He'd been preaching and counseling folks for a few years now, so he should know how to help her. The only problem was, most of those he'd helped weren't as appealing as young Glenna Moore. At least none had conjured up the protective feelings he was experiencing right now. Was there more to this than just concern for her unfortunate circumstances?

Glenna reached her seat and stopped short. Her whole body began to shake as she bent down to pick up a deck of playing cards, lying on the bench. David figured either her father had dropped them there before his great escape or one of the other gamblers had decided to return them. Either way, the last thing Glenna needed right now was a reminder of her father's folly.

He watched her study the cards as tears welled up in her eyes. Her chin began to quiver, and like a tightly coiled spring, she suddenly released her fury. "These cards are evil! They've brought us nothing but bad luck!" With a piercing scream, Glenna dashed the cards to the floor and fell in a heap beside them.

David looked around helplessly, wondering how Glenna's display of unbridled emotions was affecting those nearby. He prayed fervently for the right words to offer in comfort. To his surprise he noticed that Alexander was still asleep, as were several other passengers. A woman and her husband, who sat two seats away, were openly staring. An elderly gentleman shrugged as though he couldn't understand what all the fuss was about. David glanced toward the back of the coach. The men who'd confronted them a few moments ago were already absorbed in another round of poker, uncaring or unaware of the hysterical young woman on the floor.

David dropped to his knees beside Glenna, then scooped up the deck of cards. "The cards in themselves are not bad," he said softly. "It's the way they're often used which causes folks to sin."

Glenna hiccupped loudly as she looked up at him, her dark eyes brimming with tears. "Those cards are the reason my daddy jumped from this train."

David stuffed the cards into his jacket pocket and gave Glenna his hand. Once she was on her feet, he offered her a drink from the canteen he'd taken out from under his bench. When she calmed down some, he helped her into her own seat and sat down beside her.

She sniffed deeply as he handed her the handkerchief he'd pulled from another one of his pockets. "Thank you. You're very kind."

He smiled in response. "You know, Glenna, the deck of cards can have a double meaning."

"It c–can?"

He nodded and pulled the cards back out of his pocket. "I've been thinking about using cards such as these for one of my upcoming sermons. It might help some who are more familiar with worldly ways to better understand the Bible."

Glenna's interest was obviously piqued, for she tipped her head slightly to study the cards.

David fanned the deck and retrieved the ace. "This stands for *one* and reminds me of one God, who loves us all." When she made no response, he continued. "Now the two makes me think about the fact that the Bible is divided into two parts—the Old and New Testament." David withdrew the three of hearts. "When I see the three, I'm reminded of the Triune God—Father, Son, and Holy Spirit."

"And the four?" Glenna asked, touching a fingertip to the four of clubs.

"Four stands for the four evangelists—Matthew, Mark, Luke, and John." He held up the five of spades next. "Five makes me think of the five wise virgins who trimmed the lamp."

Glenna's forehead wrinkled. She obviously knew little or nothing about the Bible.

"The six of hearts is a reminder that God created the world in six days," David said. "On the seventh day, God rested." He tapped the seven of diamonds with his thumb.

"And the eight? What does it stand for?" she asked, leaning closer to David. In fact, she was so close that he could smell the faint aroma of her rosewater cologne.

David drew back slightly, afraid he would lose track of his thoughts if he didn't put a safe distance between them. "Eight represents the eight righteous persons God saved during the great flood. There was Noah, his wife, their three sons, and their wives."

Glenna nodded. "Mrs. Olsen, a woman who ran the boardinghouse where Daddy and I once stayed, often told Bible stories. I wasn't that interested then, but I do remember her telling about Mr. Noah and the big boat."

David chuckled. "Guess that's about right, though I've never heard it put quite that way before." He tapped the nine of spades with one finger. "This one makes me think of lepers. There were ten of them, and when Jesus healed them all, only one of the ten bothered to even thank Him. The other nine neglected to do so."

Glenna frowned. "Jesus healed men with leprosy?"

"Yes, and He made many others well, too."

"What does the ten stand for?"

"The ten represents the Ten Commandments, which were God's law. He gave the laws to the children of Israel through His servant Moses." David picked up the king of hearts. "This one reminds me of one special King. . .the One who died for each of us so we could have the gift of salvation and forgiveness from our sins."

Glenna chewed thoughtfully on her bottom lip but said nothing.

"The queen," David continued, "makes me think of the virgin, Mary, who bore our Savior, Jesus Christ."

"There's one card left," Glenna said, pointing to the jack of diamonds. "What does that stand for?"

"This card," David said, emphasizing each word, "represents the devil himself."

CHAPTER 5

Glenna's brown eyes grew as huge as flapjacks. "The devil?" she rasped. "Mrs. Olsen said the devil is man's worst enemy."

"Mrs. Olsen was right." David shuffled the cards thoroughly and held up the deck. "These can be used in a bad way, by the devil, or they can serve to remind us of the fact that there truly is a God and He loves us very much."

Glenna blinked rapidly. "God could never love someone like me."

"That's not true," David was quick to say. "Why would you even think such a thing?"

"My daddy was a gambler. He cheated people out of their money."

David shrugged. "That was your father's sin, not yours."

"But—but, sometimes I covered for him. I often told lies in order to protect him. Daddy was all I had. He watched out for me, and I took care of him." Her eyes pooled with fresh tears. "Some days, when we had no money, I begged or stole things. Daddy's gone now, and I'm all alone with no way to support myself. I hate stealing, but I may not have any other choice."

"You're not alone," David argued. "God's with you, and so am I. You don't need to lie or steal."

Her eyes drifted shut as she drew in a shuddering breath. "You're here now, but you have your own life. My ticket only takes me to Granger, Wyoming. When the train stops there, I'll be forced to get off. You'll go on and forget you ever met me."

David swallowed hard. She was right, of course. He did have a life—obligations to the church in Idaho City where he'd been asked to pastor. He could hardly take Glenna with him. Besides the fact that he barely knew Glenna Moore, she was not a Christian. By her own lips she'd admitted she was a sinner.

"He that is without sin among you, let him first cast a stone at her." The scripture passage from the book of John reverberated in David's head. He, of all people, had no right to point an accusing finger at anyone. Not after all he'd done in the past. He wondered if Glenna might question him about his earlier days now that she'd revealed some of hers.

"Your silence only confirms what I said," Glenna moaned. "Once we part ways, you'll never think of me again."

David knew that wasn't true. Though he'd only known the

young woman a few hours, she'd made a lasting impression. He turned slightly in his seat so he was looking her full in the face. "I assure you, Glenna, you are not a woman to be easily forgotten."

He resisted the urge to kiss away the tears streaming down her flushed cheeks. Instead of acting on impulse though, he merely reached out and took her hand, giving it a gentle squeeze. "Would it be agreeable for me to share some passages from the Bible with you? I believe God's Word will act as a healing balm, if you're willing to let it."

For a moment she said nothing, her eyes shut and her breathing labored. Finally she spoke. "I suppose it would be all right. I have nowhere else to turn, and all the steam has left me. . .like vapor rising from wet boots."

"There is only one place to turn. God's love can ease your pain." David removed a small Bible from his pocket and began to read some scripture verses pertaining to man's sin and the need for salvation. Then he went on to read the account of Christ's death and resurrection. "It's about as clear as cold water, Glenna. You can be released from sins by a simple prayer of faith."

"I–I don't know how to talk to God. I used to pray when I was very young—when my mother was still alive, but I haven't uttered a prayer since her death. I wouldn't even know how."

"I'll help you, Glenna. I can lead you through the sinner's prayer."

She drew in a deep breath. "Sinner—yes, that's what I am."

"We've all sinned and come short of God's glory," David

murmured. He admired her willing spirit. He wished everyone he preached to would be so eager to admit their shortcomings.

Glenna had never known such a feeling of freedom as when she finished her heartfelt prayer and confession of sin. A new creature, that's what she felt like now that she'd asked God's forgiveness and accepted Jesus as her Savior. She didn't have her real daddy anymore, but David had reminded her that the heavenly Father would always be with her.

She brushed an errant tear from her cheek and sniffed deeply. God's Spirit might be here, but physically she was still alone. Her ticket would only take her as far as Granger. Then what? Daddy had all their money. Glenna had nothing but the clothes on her back and a few more personal belongings in her suitcase. *I may have my sins forgiven,* she mused, *but I'm sure in a fine fix!*

"For a lady who's just been reborn, you look a bit down in the mouth."

David's deep, mellow voice drew Glenna out of her musings, and she shifted in her seat. "I'm glad I found Jesus, but it doesn't solve my immediate problem."

He lifted one eyebrow in question.

Her shoulders drooped with anguish and a feeling of hopelessness. "Daddy's gone, and I have no money—only a train ticket to Granger."

"Do you have any other family?"

She shook her head. "Mama died giving birth to my

brother. He died, too. That's when Daddy started drinking and gambling. He never mentioned any relatives either."

"What did your father do before that?"

Glenna had only been five at the time, but she still remembered. "Daddy used to run a mercantile up in Sioux City, Nebraska. We had a house of our own and everything."

David offered her a sympathetic look. "After your mother died, did your father sell his home and business?"

She nodded. "He sold out to the first man to make an offer."

"And then?"

"We left Sioux City and traveled from town to town. Daddy gambled in order to make a living, and I remained in the care of the boardinghouse keepers when he was gone."

"Did the women who ran the boarding homes educate you?" he asked.

Her forehead wrinkled. "Educate me? In what way?"

He smiled. "The three Rs—reading, writing, and arithmetic. Your manner of speech indicates that you are not uneducated."

Glenna shrugged. "We never stayed anywhere long enough for me to go to school with other children. Daddy was an educated man though. He always took time out to teach me reading and sums." Lost in memories, she stared down at her hands until they blurred out of focus. She'd always felt as if Daddy loved her. At least until today when he'd jumped off the train. How did he think she could care for herself? Why hadn't Daddy ever gotten a *real* job so he could be a *real* father?

A shallow sigh escaped Glenna's lips as she continued her story. "Once, when I was about ten years old, I thought Daddy might actually change."

"In what way?"

"He met a lady. I think she really loved him."

David smiled. "Many a good woman has been responsible for helping tame a man." He patted his jacket pocket, where he'd replaced the small Bible. "Of course, no one but God can ever really change a person's heart."

Glenna grimaced. "Daddy needed Jesus. Not even Sally Jeffers could heal his hurting heart. When she started making demands, Daddy packed our bags, and we left Omaha for good."

"Demands? What kind of demands did she make?"

"Asking him to settle down, get a job, and marry her." Glenna's eyes clouded with fresh tears, and she turned her head toward the window. There was no point in talking about all this now. Daddy hadn't married Sally, and he sure enough hadn't settled down. She drew in a deep breath. Life was so unfair.

David shifted uneasily in his seat as he glanced across the aisle at the poet whose nose was stuck in a book. The events of the last hour had been a bit too much. . .even for someone like himself. Maybe he should have remained in his seat, listening to Alexander go on and on about his writing and many ailments. Perhaps he shouldn't have involved himself in Glenna's life at all. The pastor part of him was as pleased as honey that she'd responded to his invitation to accept Christ as her Savior. The only fly in the ointment was the fact that Glenna's father was gone, and she had no other family to turn to. The man part of him felt responsible for someone who obviously could not care for herself. How could David abandon this woman? Glenna had relied on her father all these years, and she really needed someone now that he was gone.

David's thoughts drifted to the letter he kept tucked in an inside jacket pocket—the letter from the deacon at his new church. The congregation at Idaho City Community Church thought their new pastor was married. If he showed up without a wife, it could affect his standing in the church and maybe even the entire community. A wife could be a real asset in the home, as well as in the ministry.

For several moments David sat there quietly, thinking about a way to solve both of their problems. Then, impulsively he reached for Glenna's hand. "I–I've been thinking."

She turned to face him, an eager, almost childlike look on her face. "Yes?"

"I was wondering—how would you like to get married?"

CHAPTER 6

David didn't know what Glenna's reaction to his question might be. He thought she would probably say she wanted to think about it awhile. After all, they'd only known each other a few hours. The last thing he'd expected was for Glenna to throw herself into his arms, but that's exactly what she did.

"Yes, yes, I'll marry you!" Glenna sobbed. "Thank you, David. Thank you so much!"

Just as she pulled away, the train gave a sudden lurch, and David nearly fell off the bench. He gripped the edge of his seat to steady himself. The jolt was enough to get him thinking straight, and the sudden realization of his surprising proposal hit him full in the face. What had he been thinking? Glenna was no doubt in shock over her father's unexpected actions.

She probably only agreed to marry him because she wasn't rational right now.

David glanced her way. She was looking at him as though nothing was wrong. He had to admit, he was intrigued with the young woman, and he did find her beauty to his liking. There was another concern though. What was he was going to do with a wife he barely knew?

The hint of a smile tweaked Glenna's lips. "I know what you're thinking."

"You do?"

She nodded soberly. "You think I accepted your proposal too readily." Before David could respond, she rushed on. "I know we don't really know each other yet, but I'm sure this will work out for both of us. I'm all alone now, and I need a man." She leaned over close to him and whispered, "I will be a good wife. I promise."

David swallowed hard. Glenna Moore was pleasant and rather easy to talk to, but was this the right thing for either of them? Another concern he had was over her ability to fulfill the role of a preacher's wife. She'd only been a Christian a few hours. What did she really know about God's ways or the expectations which would no doubt be placed upon her?

"When will we get married, and who will perform the ceremony?" she asked, breaking into his troubling thoughts.

"A close friend of mine is a minister. He lives in Granger, Wyoming, so we can get married when the trains stops there."

The mention of Granger caused Glenna's heart to ache. Daddy had a friend living there, too. That's why he'd purchased their tickets to Granger. *How ironic,* she thought. *Soon I'll be leaving Nebraska far behind and marrying a man I've only just met. Then we'll be going to Idaho City, where I'll begin a whole new life as a pastor's wife.* Glenna sucked in her breath and pressed her nose against the dust-covered window. It wasn't as if she had many other choices right now. Daddy wouldn't be going to Granger or meeting up with his friend. Daddy was dead—probably crushed under the iron wheels of the train. Glenna had to think about her own needs now, and Reverend David Green was willing to take care of her. Getting married may not be the perfect situation, but at least she had somewhere to go and someone to look out for her.

Daddy cared more about himself than he did me, so now I'll do what I think is best, Glenna fumed. She bit back the bile of bitterness threatening to strip away her newfound faith. She was no longer Daddy's girl, and she never would be again.

David and Glenna spent the next few days learning a bit more about one another. He shared a seat with her during the day and slept beside his chum, Alexander, at night.

The eccentric poet often complained about the feeble illumination of the small oil lamps, glimmering at intervals along the walls of their car. At least there was enough light for David to keep an eye on Glenna. Once they were married, he would worry a whole lot less about her safety. That wouldn't stop him from worrying about his new ministry, however. Was he really ready to take on the responsibility of full-time pastoring? From what he'd learned so far, Glenna had experienced a lot of pain and emotional trauma in her past. Her newfound faith was weak yet, although she did seem eager to learn. While David felt it was God's leading that caused him to propose marriage, he could only hope and pray that she would be an asset and not a hindrance to his calling.

David glanced over at Glenna, sitting beside him now. It was another warm day, and she was fanning herself with one hand as she stared down at his Bible, lying in her lap. He was pleased that she'd asked to read the scriptures. As a new Christian, she needed to be fed with the bread of life.

"Would you care for a paper, sir?" the freckle-faced news butcher asked as he sauntered up the aisle, peddling his wares.

"I believe I will take one," David answered with a friendly smile. "I can catch up on the local news and help my lady friend to cool off at the same time."

The young boy wrinkled his forehead, but agreeably he gave David a newspaper.

As soon as he'd paid the lad, David got right down to business. He glanced quickly through the paper and found the page full of advertisements. He ripped it out, then began folding the sheet, accordion-style, until he'd made a suitable fan. When he finished, he handed it to Glenna with a smile. "Here, this might work better than your hand."

Glenna reached for the handmade contraption and immediately began to fan her face. "Ah, much better. Thank you."

"You're welcome," he said with a wink. *I wonder if she'll always be so easy to please. It gives me pleasure to make her happy. Maybe my worries about our future are totally unfounded.*

The conductor moved swiftly down the aisle, calling, "Next stop. . .Granger, Wyoming!"

As the train slowed, then jerked to an abrupt halt, Glenna felt her whole body begin to tremble. This was where she and Daddy were supposed to be getting off. This was where they would have begun a new life, in a new town, with new people—and the same old problems of Daddy's gambling and erratic drinking.

That wasn't going to happen though. Instead of searching for a suitable boardinghouse, Glenna and David would be seeking out a preacher. From the moment Glenna said "I do," her life would never be the same. Could she really go through with this crazy plan to marry a man she barely knew? But what other choice did she have? She had no money, no job, and no place to go. David offered security and a home. He was a good-looking man, not to mention pleasant and easygoing. He'd shown no signs of a temper or even any bad habits. *David would be easy to love,* she thought wistfully. *But can he ever love me? I'm a gambler's daughter, and I've only recently found forgiveness for my sins. What if I do or say something to embarrass David in front of his new congregation? What if I don't measure up?*

David grabbed his suitcase, and Glenna carried hers. He reached for Glenna's free hand, and the two of them picked their way down the narrow aisle toward the door. "Everything will be fine. You'll see," he whispered.

When they stepped inside the church, a middle-aged man with bright-red hair and a mustache to match greeted David with a warm smile and a hearty handshake. "My friend, it's so good to see you." His gaze lit on Glenna. "And who is this lovely creature?"

David slipped an arm around Glenna's waist, and her face turned crimson. "Pastor Jim Hunter, this is Glenna Moore. We plan to get married and want you to perform the ceremony." He grinned sheepishly. "That is, if you're willing and have the time."

Jim slapped David on the back. "For you, I always have time." He glanced at Glenna again but spoke to David. "I'm surprised to see you. I thought you were on the way to your new pastorate."

David knew his old friend well. The look on Jim's face said volumes. He was a lot more curious about the sudden appearance of David's fiancée than he was about his whereabouts. He knew, too, that Jim wasn't about to perform any marriage ceremony until he'd heard the details of this unplanned stop in Granger.

"If Alice is at home, maybe Glenna could go next door and freshen up a bit," David suggested.

Jim nodded. "She's home, and I'm sure my dear wife would be most happy to meet Glenna. She'll no doubt offer us all some refreshments. Then Glenna can bathe and rest awhile." He began moving toward the church's front door. "I'll walk the two of you over there, we'll say howdy to Alice, then David and I can come back here for a little chat while you get ready for the wedding. How's that sound?"

Glenna smiled and tipped her head. "I'm coated with dust from head to toe, so a bath sounds absolutely wonderful."

A short time later, they were all at the parsonage, sitting around a huge wooden table. A slightly plump, middle-aged Alice was happily playing hostess. After a cup of hot coffee and a slice of gingerbread, the men excused themselves to go back over to the church.

David wasted no time telling his friend the story that led up to his betrothal, and soon the two men found themselves on their knees in front of the altar. While Pastor Jim hadn't actually condoned David's unconventional behavior, he didn't lecture him either. Prayers went up on David's behalf, and both men beseeched the Lord for young Glenna and her new role as a minister's wife. David felt certain that Alice was probably giving his wife-to-be a few pointers as well.

Glenna felt her eyelids flutter as she forced a mind full of doubts to concentrate fully on the words Pastor Hunter was saying. She glanced nervously at her groom and sucked in her breath while he offered a reassuring smile. David had shaved off his beard and bathed before the wedding. His dark hair was still slightly damp, and as he stepped closer, the clean, fresh smell of soap assaulted her senses. This man she was about to marry was a handsome one indeed! But was she worthy of such a man? Her past life had been full of sin and lies—being forced to move from one town to another, watching Daddy drink and gamble, then making excuses for his disgusting behavior.

Glenna glanced down at the pale yellow gown she'd changed into after her bath. Made of pure silk, with a touch of lace at the neck and sleeves, it was the only nice thing she owned anymore. When she looked to her left, Alice Hunter, who stood as her witness, smiled sweetly. To David's right was Richard Hunter, the pastor's sixteen-year-old son, who was acting as David's attester. There were no flowers or music, and no one else was in the audience to share in this unusual yet auspicious occasion. Pastor Hunter stood before them, holding a Bible in his hands and wearing a solemn expression on his rotund face. As he shared several scriptures and some insights on marriage, it was obvious to Glenna that he took his job quite seriously.

A surge of panic rushed through her veins, and she nibbled on the inside of her cheek, wondering if she could really go through with this wedding. It was too late for second thoughts, though, so she forced herself to concentrate on the remainder of the ceremony.

"And now, whom God has joined together as one, let no man put asunder. I do here and now pronounce them to be man and wife," the minister said in a booming voice. "David, you may kiss your bride."

Glenna swallowed hard, steeling herself for what was to come. It was done. She was married to Reverend David Green. Would her husband's kiss be as gentle as his melodic voice? Would it send shivers of delight up her spine, causing her knees to go weak? She'd seen many women swoon after being kissed by a man, yet she'd never experienced any such thing herself. In fact, except for her father's quick pecks, Glenna had never known any man's lips.

Much to her surprise, and yes, even to her disappointment, David merely bent his head and brushed a fleeting kiss across her cheek. She was sure he had his reasons for marrying her, but love was obviously not one of them. *Does he find me unattractive or too unappealing to kiss me on the mouth?* she cried inwardly. *Did he marry me only out of obligation?*

Taking her by surprise, David bent down and whispered in Glenna's ear, "You make a beautiful bride."

Self-consciously, she lifted a hand to touch the soft curl that lay next to her ear. She'd pulled her long hair away from her face and secured it with the tortoise shell combs she often wore. However, unruly curls had a mind of their own, and a few had managed to escape.

"How would you like to have dinner in the hotel dining room before we check into our room?" David asked.

Her head jerked up. "Hotel? Are we spending the night in Granger?"

A soft chuckle escaped his lips. "Of course. There won't be

another train heading west until midday tomorrow."

Glenna nodded, feeling suddenly foolish and more than a bit flustered.

A short time later, David and Glenna said good-bye to Pastor Hunter, his wife, and their son. Soon they were seated at a table for two in the Hotel Granger's dining room. A gold-colored tablecloth graced with a cut glass vase full of daisies created a cozy, yet romantic scene.

Glenna had been subjected to some luxuries over the course of her eighteen years, but that was only when Daddy had been winning big. *Winning or cheating?* a little voice niggled at the back of her mind. *Did Daddy ever win any money in a fair game of cards?*

"What appeals to you?" David asked, breaking into her disconcerting thoughts.

She shrugged and stared blankly at the menu lying before her. "Whatever you're planning to have is fine."

When the waitress came, David placed for each of them an order for pot roast with potatoes and carrots on the side, along with a plate of fresh greens. They had coffee and tall glasses of water to drink, and a basket of freshly baked bread was brought before the main part of the meal.

"You seem rather quiet and withdrawn this evening," David noted with a look of concern. "Is everything all right? You're not having second thoughts about marrying me, are you?"

Glenna took a sip of coffee, then glanced at him over the rim of her cup. "It's not that. I'm just missing Daddy. If he hadn't jumped to his death, the two of us would have been here in Granger right now. This is where we'd planned to get off the train, you know."

David reached across the table and placed a gentle hand on top of hers. "I know you're still grieving, but remember, you have a new life with me now. We have a church and people waiting for us in Idaho City."

Glenna stared into his green eyes, so sympathetic and full of understanding. She swallowed past the lump in her throat and was about to reply when some boisterous voices caught her attention. Her gaze darted to the left. Two men were heading toward their table, arms draped across each other's shoulders, bodies swaying carelessly.

One of the men was looking directly at Glenna, and her mouth dropped open. Disbelieving her eyes, she looked down at the table then quickly back again. *Daddy?*

CHAPTER 7

Daddy's eyes glazed over, and he stared at Glenna as though he'd seen a ghost. "Glenna? Baby, is that you?"

Trembling, she could only nod. This had to be some kind of a dream. She'd seen Daddy jump from that train. Even if by some miracle he had survived the fall, there was no way he could have made it to Granger on his own steam—not to mention as quickly as the train had brought them there.

"Mr. Moore, we thought you were dead," David said, scraping his chair away from the table but still remaining seated.

"It would take a lot more than bailing off a train and rolling down a prickly embankment to kill someone as ornery as me," Daddy replied with a hearty laugh.

"But—but—how did you get here?" Glenna stammered.

"Some good folks came by in a wagon and picked me up." Daddy leaned against his friend for support and riveted David with a hard gaze.

David's face was a mask of suspicion, and Glenna noticed the muscle in his cheek had begun to twitch. "I hardly think a wagon could have beat the train here, Mr. Moore," he said evenly.

"And what about your injuries?" Glenna interjected. "Surely you must have been hurt after that fall."

Her father grinned and gave his goatee a few tugs. "I was kind of banged up but not too much worse for the wear." He took a few steps closer to their table, then leaned his weighty arms on the corner nearest Glenna. "Those folks with the wagon had an extra horse. They were kind enough to let me borrow it. That's how I made such good time."

For the first time, the man beside Daddy spoke up. "That's right. My old friend Garret galloped into town yesterday afternoon, and we've been havin' ourselves a good old time ever since." He pounded Glenna's father on the back, causing them both to wobble unsteadily.

"Yep," Daddy agreed. "Alvin and I go way back."

Glenna knew Alvin must be the friend Daddy had planned to link up with when they arrived in Granger. From the looks of things, Daddy cared more about his drinking partner than he did her. He hadn't even asked about her, nor had he seemed that interested in the fact that she was sitting in the hotel dining room having dinner with a man.

Swaying slightly, Daddy leaned over and stared David

right in the eye. "Say, you're that preacher fellow who was on the train, aren't ya?"

David nodded and opened his mouth, but Glenna cut him right off. "David's my husband now, Daddy. We were married today. . .by a *preacher* here in Granger. . .in a *church.*" Why Glenna was emphasizing the words preacher and church, she wasn't sure. Maybe it was to be certain Daddy knew the marriage was legal and binding, and there was nothing he could do about it. If he cared so little about Glenna that he would jump off the train and leave her all alone, then he had no right to interfere in her life now.

"You're what?" Daddy bellowed.

She lifted her chin and held his steady gaze. "I'm a married woman."

Daddy's fist came down hard against the table, jostling the silver and nearly upsetting the vase of daisies. "You can't be married!"

David jumped to his feet, quickly skirting the table to stand beside Glenna. He placed one hand on her trembling shoulder. "Glenna's my wife. We'll be leaving on the train tomorrow, heading for my new pastorate in Idaho City."

Daddy's face reddened further, and he shook his fist in front of David's nose. "Glenna is *my* daughter, and you can't have her! She's staying here, not traipsing off to Idaho with some high-and-mighty Bible-thumper!"

Glenna's ears burned, and her eyes stung with unwanted tears. Her father and her new husband were arguing over her. She'd been Daddy's girl for eighteen years. She'd only been

Reverend David Green's wife a few hours. Anxiety gnawed at her insides, but she knew she had a choice to make. Who should she stay with? Her chin quivered as she considered her options. "David is my husband. I'm going with him."

David tensed protectively when Garret Moore grabbed Glenna's arm. "Have you taken leave of your senses? You're my daughter, and I've always met your needs."

"The way you did on the train?" David asked between clenched teeth.

"Glenna wouldn't have a father right now if I hadn't jumped," Garret snarled, though he did release his grip on Glenna's arm. "Those card sharks were gonna kill me. I had to make a quick escape, and I figured I'd make it to Granger, then meet up with Glenna when the train stopped here. How was I to know she'd go and do something so foolish as gettin' hitched up with the likes of you?"

David stepped closer to Garret, nearly knocking him into his buddy, Alvin. "I'm sorry about all your troubles, Mr. Moore, but if you hadn't been gambling in the first place—"

"Don't you go preachin' at me, sonny!" Garret shouted. "I've made a fair-enough living at my trade, and my daughter's never done without." He perused Glenna a few moments and frowned. "Are ya comin' with me or not?"

David's spirits slid straight to his boots. What if Glenna had changed her mind? What if he had no wife to take to his new pastorate after all? Relief bubbled up in his chest when she shook her head, but it ripped at David's heartstrings to see her so shaken and torn. He knew she'd always been "Daddy's girl," and deciding to stay with him rather than go with her father could not have been an easy decision.

Garret shrugged his shoulders. "Suit yourself, daughter, but if you change your mind, I'll be at Mrs. O'Leary's boardinghouse." With that, he grabbed his pal's arm and practically pushed him out of the room.

As Glenna stood staring out their hotel-room window, her thoughts became a tangled web of confusion. She hadn't been this upset since Daddy jumped off the train three days ago. It was hard to find any joy over her marriage, especially after learning that her father was alive. Knowing that she and David would be leaving tomorrow and she'd probably never see Daddy again didn't help her mood either. Even if she and David ever returned to Granger for a visit with David's friend, what were the chances that Daddy would be there? Daddy never stayed anywhere very long. He'd get bored and decide to move on to the next town. Or someone would catch him cheating, and he'd be run out of town with the threat of jail or a bullet in his back.

Glenna wished Daddy could find forgiveness for his sins and know the sweet sense of peace she'd found by asking Jesus into her heart. She knew there was nothing she could do for Daddy now but pray.

Forcing all thoughts of her father aside, Glenna concentrated on her new husband. David had seemed a bit distant since they'd left the hotel dining room and come upstairs to their room. Was he sorry he'd married her? Had Daddy's unexpected appearance marred their future? Maybe David thought she really wanted to go with Daddy and was only staying with him out of obligation. Despite the fact that she hardly knew David Green, Glenna was certain of one thing—her husband was a good person. He was a man of God, not some drunk who thought nothing of gambling away his money as though it were no more than a jar of glass marbles.

Goose bumps erupted on Glenna's arms as David stepped up behind her, wrapping his comforting arms around her waist. She'd thought he was still sitting in the cane-backed chair across the room, reading his Bible.

"Glenna, I think we should talk." David's words came out in a whisper, caressing her ear with the warmth of his breath.

She leaned into him, relishing the closeness of his body and the way his embrace made her feel so protected. She drew in a deep breath, letting it out in a lingering sigh. She knew it was ridiculous because they barely knew one another, but she had fallen hopelessly in love with this man. The question was, did David return her feelings, or was he merely being kind? Did David see her as a woman he could love or just a needy person he felt obligated to care for?

"I appreciate your being willing to marry me," she murmured. "I know it wasn't in your plans, but I'm very grateful."

"I think we need to talk," David repeated.

She nodded mutely and allowed him to take her hand. He led her over to the bed, and they both took a seat. "I realize seeing your father today was quite a shock," he said softly.

"I never thought he could survive such a fall," she admitted.

"Glenna, I—"

"He abandoned me on that train," she said, cutting him off. "Now Daddy thinks I should abandon you."

"And would you?"

Unwanted tears rolled down her cheeks. "Daddy doesn't care about me anymore." She sniffed deeply. "And I care nothing for him."

David's fingers clasped her own, and warmth spread quickly up her arms as she savored the feel of his gentle touch. She relished the feeling of safety she had with David and was confident she could trust him never to abandon her the way Daddy had.

"You must forgive your father, Glenna," David said.

She shrugged. The motion was all she could manage, given the circumstances. Talking about her father was too painful right now. Besides, she didn't want to forgive Daddy. She was angry with him. Could it be that she was staying with David only to get even with Daddy?

David draped an arm around her shoulders, pulling her close. He bent his head slightly, and she was sure he was about to kiss her. To her disappointment, he pulled away suddenly and stood up. "We'd best settle down for the night and get some sleep." His words trailed off in a yawn. "You can have the bed, and I'll sleep on the floor." He dipped his head, refusing to make eye contact with her. "Good night, Glenna."

Glenna awoke the following morning feeling as though her head had been stuffed with a wad of cotton. Last night had been her wedding night, and she hadn't slept well. Visions of Daddy and David had danced through her head like storm clouds. Did either of them love her at all? Did anyone love her? David said God loved her, but God was a spirit. How could He ever meet all her needs?

She was thankful when they went down to breakfast and found that Daddy was nowhere around. Since David obviously didn't love her, she'd actually been having some thoughts about staying in Granger with Daddy. If she saw him again, she might weaken. Glenna knew in her heart that a marriage without love would be preferable to her previous life as a gambler's daughter. She'd made up her mind. As difficult as it would be to board that train, she was going to Idaho City with her husband!

A short time later, she and David were seated on a wooden bench in front of the train station. Glenna glanced about, tugging nervously on the strings of her handbag. *I'm doing the right thing,* she kept telling herself. *I am a new creature in Christ now. I can never go back to my old way of life, no matter how much I might miss Daddy.*

"You look pale. Are you all right?" David asked, eyeing her with a look of concern.

She gave a slight nod and kept her voice strong. "I'll be fine once we board the train."

Gazing down at the open Bible in his lap, David offered a half smile. "I hope so."

When a familiar voice called out her name, Glenna jerked her head up. Daddy was heading their way. She jumped to her feet, clenching her fists in anticipation for what he might say or do.

"Glenna, I'm so glad I caught you before the train left," Daddy panted. "I have something to give you."

David was at her side now, and she felt his hand at the small of her back. "We have no need of tainted money, Mr. Moore," he said evenly.

Her father laughed, shaking his head and reaching into his jacket pocket. "It's not money I wish to give. I want my daughter to have her mother's wedding ring." He held up a delicate gold band and handed it to Glenna.

She stood there, mouth hanging open and eyes filled with tears. "This was Mama's ring?"

His head bobbed up and down. "I've been holding it until you got married. Please take the ring, Glenna. Your mother would have wanted you to have it."

Glenna glanced briefly at David. His brows were furrowed, and his lips were set in a fine line. "I had no ring to give you on our wedding day," he mentioned. "I think it would be a good thing if you wore your mother's ring, don't you?"

She accepted the gift then, letting her father slip it on the ring finger of her left hand. The fact that Daddy had sought her out, offering such a fine present and not making a scene about her being married or going to Idaho City made Glenna feel guilty for her bitter feelings. She swallowed past the lump in her throat. "Thank you, Daddy. I'll cherish this ring for the rest of my life."

Daddy's eyes filled with tears. She'd never seen him cry before and was taken by surprise. He opened his mouth as if to say something, but the words never came. With no warning whatsoever, an ear-piercing shot rang out. Daddy dropped like a sack of grain at Glenna's feet.

CHAPTER 8

Glenna screamed, then collapsed to the ground beside her father's body. Daddy wasn't breathing. Dark blood oozed from a bullet wound that had obviously penetrated his back and gone clear through to his chest.

David spun around and raced off toward the gunman. There was chaos everywhere. Some nearby folks screeched in terror, others ran about calling for help, and a few stayed to offer comfort to a very distraught Glenna.

It was inconceivable, but in the short span of a few days, she'd lost her father twice. First when he'd jumped from the moving train and now from a bullet in the back!

"How could this have happened?" she sobbed. "How could God be so cruel?" She observed the faces staring down at her with apparent pity. They were all faces of strangers. Where was David? Had he abandoned her, too?

Glenna sat in her seat, ramrod stiff, barely aware of the irritating sway of the train and not noticing any of her surroundings. She felt cold and empty inside. Even the warm hand placed upon her own did nothing to console her anguished soul. Everything was so final. Daddy was gone, and there had been no chance to make amends or even say a proper good-bye. There hadn't been any possibility for her to witness about God's redeeming love either. She'd failed Daddy, and God had failed her. She would probably let David down as well. How could she possibly go to Idaho City and be a pastor's wife when she felt so dead inside? Why had she ever agreed to this marriage of convenience in the first place? She'd been foolish to get caught up in the silly notion that her life could be better. Her hopes and dreams for the future had been buried, right along with Daddy's lifeless body. The words Pastor Hunter said at the grave site this morning had done little to comfort Glenna's aching heart.

She glanced down at the golden band on her left hand. It was all she had left of her mother, and giving it to her had been the last good thing Daddy had ever done. Maybe it was the *only* good thing he'd ever done.

Glenna's thoughts swept her painfully back to yesterday. She could still see Daddy racing eagerly toward her. In her mind's eye, she saw his apologetic smile, heard the words of love, and felt his warm hand as he slipped Mama's ring onto her finger.

Glenna tried to stop what came next, but it was to no avail. She could hear that fatal gunshot echoing in her head as though it were happening again. The image of Daddy's pale face and blood-soaked shirt would be inscribed in her brain for as long as she lived. She had known he was gone, even before the doctor came along and pronounced him dead.

There had been no train trip that afternoon. Instead, she and David spent the next several hours in the sheriff's office, giving him the sketchy details of the unexpected shooting. David had seen the murderer, and he'd even chased after him. The gunman had vanished as quickly as he'd appeared. Quite possibly her father's killer would never be caught or punished.

David had sent a telegram to one of his church members, letting him know they were going to be detained another day and, Lord willing, would leave for Idaho City the following afternoon. Reverend Hunter agreed to do the graveside service for Daddy the next morning, and they would be spending another night in the Granger Hotel.

Glenna swallowed against the lump in her throat. Their second night had been even worse than the first. David slept on the floor again, and she'd refused to even look at him or say a single word. There was a part of her that blamed David for all this. Had he not suggested they get married, she would have simply gotten off the train in Granger, gone looking for a job, and sooner or later would have run into Daddy. If she hadn't married David, Daddy might still be alive.

As frustration and exhaustion closed in like a shroud,

Glenna shut her eyes. Leaning her head against the window, she let much-needed sleep claim her weary body.

David watched the rhythmic rise and fall of Glenna's steady breathing. He was glad she'd finally given in to sleep. She had been too distraught to sleep much of the night before and had withdrawn into a cocoon of silence. His heart ached for her, yet he had no idea how to draw Glenna out. It would probably be most appropriate to leave her alone for now, letting grief run its course in whatever way she chose. During his ministerial training, David had been taught about the various stages of bereavement a person went through when losing a loved one. The first was shock. Later came denial or a great sense of loss, often accompanied by depression. Glenna appeared to be in the first stage right now, which was no doubt for the best. David needed time to read the scriptures and pray, asking for God's wisdom in helping her through this grieving process.

It was interesting, he noted, that she hadn't been nearly as despondent when her father jumped off the train and she thought he'd been killed. Perhaps this "second death" was more traumatic since Garret had been murdered in cold blood, right in front of her. His death was final. No more wondering if he might have survived, and no more anger because he'd taken his own life. This time he'd been killed by an assassin, plain and simple. Who the man was, why he'd fired the fateful shot, and where he had gone was still a mystery which might never be solved. David's job as Glenna's husband was to help her through this difficult time, no matter how long it took. He owed her that much.

David ran his fingers through his sweat-soaked hair, as troubled thoughts took him back to the last two nights spent at the Hotel Granger. It had been a difficult decision, but he'd chosen to sleep on the floor, not wanting to rush his new bride into something she might not be ready for yet. Perhaps it had been a mistake to do so, but it was in the past and couldn't be changed.

He released a deep sigh and glanced over at her again. The truth was, David wasn't sure about his feelings for the sleeping woman who sat beside him. Was it love or merely a sense of obligation that invaded his senses every time she looked his way? There was no point in leading her on. They both needed more time. Time to get to know one another. Time to grow in their relationship. For some reason she hadn't asked about his past, and he hoped she wouldn't hate him once she learned the truth.

Glenna awoke from her nap feeling a bit more rested but still deeply troubled. She peeked over at David. In one hand he held his Bible; in the other was a deck of cards. They were Daddy's cards—the same ones he'd left on the seat before he jumped off the train. She'd thrown the cards on the floor, and David had retrieved them, later using the deck as some sort of parallel to things written in the Bible. Glenna was surprised to see that David still had those cards. Why hadn't he thrown them away? What would a God-fearing, Bible-teaching preacher need with a deck of cards?

David must have caught her staring at him, for he turned in his seat and smiled. "Good, you're awake. Did you rest well?"

Her only reply was a stiff nod. What did he care—this husband who slept on the floor and had spoken only a few words to her since Daddy's death?

David stuffed the Bible into his jacket pocket, but he kept the cards held firmly in one hand. With the other hand, he reached out to touch Glenna's arm. "You've been through a horrible ordeal, but in time God will heal your internal wounds."

Glenna scowled at him. "I'm not so sure. If God makes bad things happen to people, then He's no better than Daddy! How can I count on Him to heal anything?"

David averted his gaze to the deck of cards. "God doesn't *make* bad things happen to His children, Glenna. He *allows* them."

"Why? Why would a loving Father let bad things happen to His children?"

David fanned out the deck. "These cards are an example of God's love for me."

She tipped her head in question.

"I haven't told you much about my past, and you've been kind enough not to ask." He pinched the bridge of his nose and frowned. "There are some things I think you should know. Especially since I've taken you to be my wife and to share in my ministry."

"I don't understand."

David cleared his throat and shuffled the cards on his knees. "There was a time when I was no better than your father." His eyes glazed over as he stared out the window. He appeared to be transported to another time. . .another place.

Glenna waited patiently for him to come to grips with whatever he needed to say. It was hard to imagine David Green being anything like Daddy.

After several moments, David turned to look at her again. "I–uh–used to be a gambler."

Glenna's mouth dropped open, and she gasped. "You what?"

"I gambled and cheated people, just the way your father did."

Glenna felt her whole body begin to sway, and she knew it was not from the motion of the train. Her head felt light, and her vision began to blur. She needed fresh air. She had to get away from David. Bounding from her seat, Glenna started down the aisle.

"Where are you going?" David called after her. "Please come back and let me explain."

Glenna kept moving as fast as her wobbly legs would allow. By the time she reached the end of their car and had stepped through the door to the platform, Glenna was sure she was going to lose the little bit of food she'd eaten before they boarded the train.

Grasping the cold, metal railing, she leaned her head over the side and breathed deeply. Since the weather was warm and humid, it wasn't fresh air, but at least she was away from David—her gambling husband. He'd lied to her. He'd led her on and made her believe he would take care of her. David was right—he was no better than Daddy. She had no one now. A little voice in the back of her mind whispered, *You have Me, Glenna. I will never leave you, nor forsake you.*

Scalding tears streamed down her face, and she cried out in anguish, "Dear Father, is that You?"

"No, it's me! Your old man's dead." A deep, grinding voice sliced through the air like a knife.

Glenna whirled around to confront a stocky, red-faced man. He wore a patch over one eye and held a gun in his hand. She opened her mouth to scream, but it was too late to cry for help. One beefy, moist hand clamped across her mouth as the man jerked her roughly to his chest. "Where is it?" he growled. "Where's the money?"

CHAPTER 9

With the man's clammy hand planted firmly over her mouth and his foul-smelling body pressing her up against the hard railing, Glenna could neither move nor speak. She wiggled and squirmed, but it was to no avail.

"Hold still, or I'll toss ya over the side," he hissed.

Glenna stiffened, unable to understand what was going on or why. She'd come out for some air and to get away from David. She never expected something like this to happen.

The man held the tip of his derringer at Glenna's back, squishing her against the iron rail. "I'm gonna take my hand off your mouth now. If ya cry out, I'll pitch ya on over. Is that clear?"

Glenna could only nod. Tears of frustration coursed down

her flaming cheeks while icy fingers of fear crept up her spine. She'd made another unwise decision. She should have stayed in her seat and let David explain about his past life. No matter how much it hurt to hear that he'd once been a gambler, it was nothing compared to the way she was feeling now. Gripping the rail, she stood motionless, waiting for her captor to remove his hand.

In one quick motion, the man jerked his hand away, then pushed the gun tightly into her back. "I wanna know where that money is, and I need to know now!"

"Wh–wh–what money?" she stammered.

His hand went to her throat, and he gave it a warning squeeze. "Don't play coy with me. Your daddy had my money, and I saw him give it to you before he died."

"No, no, he didn't. All Daddy gave me was my mother's ring." Glenna held up her hand. "I know nothing about any money."

"Ah–hem! Is there some kind of problem here?"

Glenna turned her head toward the sound of a man's deep voice. It was the conductor. She breathed a sigh of relief. Everything would be all right now. She'd be safe, and this horrible man with putrid breath would soon be locked away in the baggage car until the train stopped at the next town. Then he'd be hauled off to jail, which was exactly where he belonged!

"Nope, there ain't no problem here," the evil man said to the conductor. His hand went to Glenna's waist, and he swiveled around, pulling her with him. "Me and the little lady was just havin' a friendly chat whilst we got us a whiff of fresh air."

Glenna felt the tip of his gun and wished it could be seen by the conductor. She nodded at the man in uniform, offering him the weakest of smiles. "Everything's fine."

The conductor hesitated, but a few seconds later he tipped his hat and opened the door to enter the car.

A sense of relief washed over Glenna, but it was quickly replaced with one of fear. The man wearing the eye patch wanted his money, and he was convinced she had it. Not knowing what else to do, Glenna sent up a quick prayer. *Help me, God. I need You now.*

David reached into his vest pocket, drew out a gold pocket watch and flipped it open to check the time. It was a little after four. Glenna had been gone nearly half an hour. How much more time did she need to cool down? David knew it wasn't her body that needing cooling though. Glenna had been madder than a wet hen when she'd stormed off without a word of explanation. Had he been a fool to believe he could divulge the secrets of his past and not have her react unfavorably? After being dragged from town to town all her life, never knowing the security of a real home, how else would Glenna have reacted? He thought she'd found a sense of peace when she accepted Jesus as her Savior. Had he undone all that by his untimely confession? *If only she'd allowed me to explain,* he fretted. *I really believed I could tell my story and make Glenna see how God changed me. I'd hoped she might even see how a simple deck of cards can be used for good, to teach others about the Lord.*

David rubbed his fingers along his chin, suddenly missing the beard he used to hide behind. *I haven't gambled in years and wouldn't dream of using marked cards now, much less cheat anyone out of their money.* He leaned to the left, trying to see up the aisle. He could see nothing through the small window of the door leading to the open platform. He glanced down at his timepiece again. If Glenna didn't return to her seat in the next five minutes, he was going out there!

Held at gunpoint, up against the railing again, Glenna felt as helpless as a pitiful baby bird caught between two cats. If only she could make the man believe she had no money. Maybe then he would leave her alone. *God, if You see me safely through this, I promise to go back to David and let him explain things about his past,* she prayed. *Perhaps David really has changed. Maybe he isn't like Daddy at all.*

Glenna leaned her head as far away from the man as possible. She could feel his hot breath against the back of her neck. She could hear his heavy, ragged breathing. "I don't know who you are, mister, and I don't understand why you think I have your money, but I can assure you—"

Slap! The man's fat hand connected to the back of Glenna's head.

Her head snapped forward. Stinging tears streamed down her burning cheeks, and she clamped her mouth shut in an effort to keep from crying out. Where was God, her Father, now? It appeared as if He had abandoned her, too.

"Garret Moore cheated me outta all my money at the gamblin' table a few nights ago," the man sputtered. "I seen him hand it over to you. Then I shot him."

Glenna gasped. So this was her father's murderer! The one David had chased. The one who'd vanished as quickly as he'd appeared. Apparently the man had followed them when they boarded the train. He'd obviously been hiding out somewhere, waiting for the chance to accost her. If she didn't give him what he wanted, there was a good chance he would kill her, too. But how could she give him what she didn't have? It was an impossible situation. Unless...

"My mother's ring is made of pure gold," she rasped. "Might I give that to you, in exchange for the money you lost?"

"I didn't lose it," he snarled. "It was stolen from me, plain and simple."

"I'm sorry about your misfortune, but I have no money, and Mama's ring..."

"Hang your mama's ring!" he bellowed. "I didn't kill a man or board this train for some stupid circle of gold that probably ain't worth half what your old man took from me." He squeezed Glenna's arm, and she winced. "Now, what's it gonna be, sister? Are ya ready to talk, or do you wanna join your daddy in death?"

Glenna opened her mouth to reply, but she was cut off by a voice she recognized. "What's going on here?"

The would-be killer whirled around, pulling Glenna with him. "This ain't none of your business! Now get back in that car, and be quick about it!"

"I'm afraid you're wrong," David said evenly. "I'm married to the woman you're holding at gunpoint. That makes it my business."

The sight of David standing there snatched Glenna's breath away, and she shot him a pleading look. David didn't seem to notice though. He was holding a Bible in one hand, and his mouth was set in a determined line. He may not love her, but he obviously cared for her safety. Perhaps she'd been wrong about him being like Daddy.

"Your little woman has somethin' that belongs to me," the sinister man growled. "I aim to get it back, so you'd better not try to interfere."

Glenna's eyes filled with fresh tears, and her voice quavered. "I don't have his money, David. The only thing Daddy gave me was my mother's ring."

"That's right. I was there when he did. Garret Moore never gave her any money at all." David waved the Bible. "I'm a minister of the Gospel. I wouldn't lie about something like this."

"Humph!" the man scoffed. "You would say that. All you Bible-thumpers want is money. Why, you'd do most anything to wangle some cash outa good folks."

"That isn't true. I'm sure David would never try to take people's money," Glenna defended. With her newfound faith in him, she offered her husband a weak smile, and he responded with one of his own.

David's gaze darted back to Glenna's captor. "I'm asking you nicely to let my wife go." He took a few steps forward, but the evil man lowered his head and charged like a billy goat. The blow caught David in the stomach, and it left him sprawled on the wooden platform, gasping for breath.

Free of the gambler for the first time, Glenna seized the opportunity at hand. With no thought for her own safety and feeling a need to help David, she began raining blows on the man's back with her fists.

At first, the fellow just stood there, grinning as though he was amused at her feeble attempts. After a few seconds, he grabbed one of Glenna's wrists and jerked her to his side. "Take one last look at your woman, preacher man, 'cause I'm about to shoot her dead if she don't tell me where that money's hid."

David struggled to sit up, then lifted the Bible over his head. "In the name of Jesus, I command you to reconsider."

Much to Glenna's surprise, the gunman dropped his weapon to the floor and extended both hands in the air.

A slight shuffling noise drew Glenna's attention off her husband's astonished face to the man standing directly behind him. The tall, brawny sheriff, wearing a gold star pinned to the front of his brown leather vest, stepped forward to apprehend his prisoner.

David stood up, and Glenna rushed into his arms, nearly knocking them both to the floor.

CHAPTER 10

With the aid of the conductor in front and David behind, Glenna stepped wearily from the train. They had finally arrived in Boise City and would be traveling by wagon to Idaho City, their final destination. The trip from Granger had taken two days, climbing steep mountains, threading their way through dark tunnels, and creeping along dizzying shelves, hundreds of feet above the river. Glenna was exhausted and wasn't relishing the bumpy ride in a hard-seated buckboard, but at least they could stop whenever they pleased, and there would be plenty of fresh air.

Their last days on the train had been rather quiet. Glenna wanted David to tell her more about his past, but he thought it best to wait until they were heading to Idaho City in the wagon. David had spent a lot of time reading his Bible and praying, and she'd done the same. Maybe it would make a difference when they did take the time to talk things out.

Glenna found a seat inside the train station, where she would wait with their luggage while David went to the livery stable for a wagon. Butterflies played tag in her stomach whenever she thought about the days ahead. Would she and David ever be able to communicate? Could she find the courage to tell him what was truly in her heart? Would their pasts always lie between them like a barbed wire fence, or could they use those terrible things to build a firm foundation for their marriage and David's ministry?

Glenna's head jerked up when David touched her arm. "Ready to go?"

She offered him a hesitant smile. "Ready as I'll ever be."

David loaded their suitcases and the supplies he'd purchased for the trip into the back of the wagon, then covered it all with a canvas tarp. He went around to help Glenna into her seat, but to his surprise, she was already sitting there with a strange look on her face. He cast her a sidelong glance as he climbed into his own seat and took up the reins. "All set?"

She merely nodded in reply.

They rode without conversation for nearly an hour, the silence broken only by the steady *clip-clop* of the horses' hooves over the rutted trail leading them northward. The warm afternoon sun beat down on their heads, and David began to pray for traveling mercies on this trip which would take a day and a half.

"The landscape here in Idaho is much different than the plains of Nebraska," Glenna said, breaking into David's prayer.

"That's right. Lots of tall, rugged hills surrounding the area."

A gentle sigh escaped her lips. "I've never been this far west. It's beautiful."

He smiled. She liked the land. That was a good sign. Yes, a very good sign.

"Will you tell me about your past now?" Glenna asked suddenly. If their marriage was ever going to work, she really did need to know more about this husband of hers, even if it wasn't all to her liking.

David tipped his head. "I suppose it is time I tell you."

Glenna leaned back in her seat, making herself as comfortable as possible, while David began his story. "I was born in Ames, Iowa. When I was sixteen, my parents and younger brother, Dan, were killed."

"What happened?"

"There was a fire. Our whole house burned down, and they were all inside."

Glenna gasped. "How awful! Were you in the house too?"

He shook his head. "I was spending the night at my cousin Jake's. I didn't even know about the fire until the next morning. I came home expecting some of Mom's delicious buttermilk flapjacks for breakfast. Instead, I found nothing but the charred remains of what used to be our home."

Even from a side view, Glenna could see the grief written on David's face. The tone of his voice was one of regret, too. She knew what it felt like to lose both her parents and a little brother. She and David had that much in common.

"What did you do after you found your house burned and knew your family was gone?" she prompted, laying a hand on his arm.

David gripped the reins a bit tighter, and a muscle in the side of his cheek began to twitch. "I lit out on my own, and I never went home again."

Glenna's mouth fell open. "But you were only sixteen. How did you—"

"Support myself?"

She nodded.

"I learned the fine art of gambling," he replied tersely. "I traveled from town to town, cheating people out of their money, lying, stealing, cursing the day I'd been born, and blaming myself for my family's deaths."

"How could you be held accountable for that? You said you weren't even at home when the fire started."

David blew out a ragged breath. "I didn't start the fire, but if I'd been there, I might have saved a life or two."

She studied him intently. "Maybe you would have been killed, too. Have you ever thought about that?"

He shrugged. "There were days when I wished I had been."

Glenna sat there awhile, letting his words sink in. Hadn't she felt the same way after Daddy was killed? Maybe it was part of the grieving process to think such thoughts. "How did you get away from the life of gambling?" she finally asked.

He turned his head and offered her a heart-melting smile. "Pastor James Hunter found me, and I found the Lord."

"He *found* you? I don't understand."

"Some men—gamblers I met on a riverboat in Mississippi—beat me up real bad and dumped me in the river. Jim was fishing nearby, and he saved me from drowning."

"But Pastor Hunter lives in Granger, Wyoming," she reminded.

David chuckled. "True, but he didn't always live there. He used to pastor a church down south."

"So, he saved your life and told you about Jesus, much like you did for me."

"That's right. I saw the light—like Paul in the Bible on his trip to Damascus. Shortly after my conversion, I felt led to become a minister. I traveled as a circuit-riding preacher for a few years, then finally went to Hope Academy in Omaha, Nebraska, for more training. That's when the church here in Idaho called me to be their full-time pastor."

"God changed your heart," she said softly. "I should have known by your actions that you were nothing like Daddy."

"Glenna, about your father. . ."

"Yes?"

"I really believe it might help if you talked about your feelings toward him."

"There's nothing to say. Daddy's dead, and the only good thing he ever did was give me this." She held up her left hand to show him her mother's wedding band.

"I believe there's some good in all men," David murmured. "After all, your father married your mother, didn't he?"

She only nodded in response.

"Through their union, you were created, and that was a good thing."

A small, whitewashed wooden structure, which David referred to as "the parsonage," stood next to a tall white church. This was to be their new home. Glenna swallowed back the lump which had formed in her throat. One week ago she had no home at all. Now, thanks to her impetuous decision to marry Reverend David Green, Glenna was about to take up residence in Idaho City—as a minister's wife, for goodness' sake. Never in a million years had she expected her life to take such a turn. Even if David didn't love her the way she loved him, she would at least have a sense of belonging.

As they stepped down from the wagon, a short, middle-aged man with a balding head came bounding out of the church. His smile stretched from ear to ear as he extended one hand toward David. "So you're the new preacher." He looked Glenna up and down, then nodded in apparent approval, grinning at her, too. "This must be the little woman. A bit younger than we expected, but I'm sure she'll fit in with some of our ladies."

David shook the man's hand. "This is my wife, Glenna. And you are—"

"Deacon Eustace Meyers," the little man said with a flutter of his eyelids. "You need anything done around the church, and I'm your man. You need a meeting called, and I'll get the word spread, quick as a wink."

Glenna bit back the laughter threatening to bubble up from her throat. She had no doubt about the ability of Deacon Meyers to get something done."

"I'll show you the house first," Eustace said, nodding toward the smaller building. "I'm sure you're wantin' to get settled in and all."

David grabbed two suitcases from the back of the wagon, and Eustace carried one of the supply boxes. Glenna followed, wondering if all David's church members were as friendly and helpful as the deacon seemed to be.

Once inside, Glenna wandered from room to room, inspecting her new home. It was small but quite serviceable. Besides the living room, there was a homey little kitchen, one bedroom downstairs, and a modest loft overhead. This would no doubt serve as David's office or perhaps be used as a guest room, should they ever have overnight company.

As David and Eustace talked about the church, which members he should get to know right away, and how many places of business were in this mining town, Glenna relished her new surroundings. She sent up a silent prayer, thanking God for being so good as to give her a place to call home. Her only concern was whether she could be the kind of wife

David needed. As long as she harbored resentment toward Daddy, Glenna knew her ability to minister to others would be impaired.

"I'll leave you two to get settled in now," she heard the deacon tell David. He moved toward the front door, then just as he was about to exit, he turned back around. "Oh, I almost forgot to give you this." He reached inside his shirt pocket and pulled out a piece of paper. "It's a telegram. . .for you, Mrs. Green."

"For me?" Glenna couldn't imagine who might be sending her a telegram.

"Are you going to read it, or should I?" Eustace asked, stepping up beside her. "I've had an eighth-grade education, you know."

"I can read it myself, thank you," Glenna replied.

The deacon nodded and stepped outside.

Glenna's hands began to tremble as she studied the telegram.

David pulled her to his side. "What's wrong? Is it bad news?"

She shook her head. "No, quite the contrary, it's good news."

"Are you going to share this good news?" he prodded.

"The telegram says there's money waiting for me. . .at the bank here in town."

"Money? From whom?"

She shrugged. "I don't know. It just says I should go to the bank and ask about a bank draft made out in my name." She moistened her lips with the tip of her tongue. "Do you think it's a joke?"

"I don't know," David replied. "I guess the only way to find out is to make a trip over to the bank. Would you like to go right now?"

She nodded. "Yes, please."

The bank president greeted them enthusiastically, stating that he and his family attended David's church and would be at the service on Sunday morning. When Glenna showed him the telegram, Mr. Paulson beamed. "Yes, indeed. I have a bank draft in my safe, made out for quite a tidy little sum. There's a note attached to it as well."

Glenna and David took seats, while Mr. Paulson went in the back to get the money in question. When he returned, he handed the legal paper to Glenna, along with a handwritten note. It was Daddy's handwriting! She'd have recognized it anywhere. But how? When?

"David, this draft is from my father," she squeaked. "The letter's from him, too. Daddy says he was once a God-fearing man. After losing Mama and my little brother, Daddy walked away from God and turned to whiskey bottles and the gambling table for comfort." She swallowed against the tide of tears threatening to spill over. "Daddy says he kept Mama's dowry all these years. He never spent any of it. . .not even when he'd gambled everything else away. When Daddy left the hotel in Granger, he decided to wire Mama's dowry money here, knowing this was where I'd be living with you."

David lifted a finger to wipe away the tears streaming down Glenna's cheeks. "There *was* some good in your father. It could be that he turned back to God before his death, too."

David's tender words and warm smile made Glenna's heart beat so fast she thought she might fall right out of her chair. She smiled through her tears. "I was Daddy's girl all my life. Now Daddy's gone, but my true Father is God. I know you're not in love with me, David, but I believe God sent you to me."

As they left the bank, Glenna leaned into David. "I love you, Pastor Green, and I'm going to try to be the best wife I can." She moved to stand in front of David, then boldly wrapped her arms around his neck. With no thought of their surroundings or who might be watching, she kissed him full on the mouth.

David responded by returning her kiss, sending a cascade of glorious shivers down her back. "I probably haven't shown it too well, but I do love you, Glenna," he whispered. "I've been asking myself for the last several days why God put us together on the same train. The answer He put in my mind kept coming back the same—we were meant for each other."

Glenna released a sigh of relief. Until this very moment, she'd never felt more loved or cherished.

"I found you, and you found God," David whispered against her ear.

"Yes, and since God is my Father, I'll always be Daddy's girl."

DEAR TEACHER

DEDICATION

To Mrs. Rueger, my favorite schoolteacher,
who encouraged me to believe in myself.

Trust in the Lord with all thine heart;
and lean not unto thine own understanding.
In all thy ways acknowledge him,
and he shall direct thy paths.
Proverbs 3:5–6

Dear Reader,

I have always appreciated teachers, but when I began doing research for this book, my admiration for those who taught in one-room schoolhouses increased a hundredfold.

Teachers who taught in one-room schoolhouses during the 1800s and early 1900s served not only as instructors but also as janitors and disciplinarians. They averaged working as many as ten hours a day and were expected to see that the building was clean and orderly at all times.

Education has changed a lot from the years of the one-room schoolhouse. The buildings are bigger, the classes are larger, and discipline is no longer of a physical nature. However, some things haven't changed—the basic curriculum of reading, writing, and arithmetic, and the need for qualified teachers.

During the days when the canals and other waterways were actively being used to transport coal and other items, the children who traveled and worked with their parents always had some time for fun. They played games such as marbles, dominoes, and checkers. Many had homemade toys, such as a spool with four nails used to weave a rope. Some little girls played with corn-husk or apple-headed dolls. Most of these children never had much more than a fourth-grade education, yet those who went to Sunday school or learned about God through their parents received a religious education that carried into their adult lives and gave them hope for the future.

Wanda

CHAPTER 1

Parryville, Pennsylvania—1890

Judith King pushed her trunk to the foot of the four-poster bed and closed the lid. She would sleep in this cozy room tonight and every night for as long as she remained in Parryville as schoolteacher at the one-room schoolhouse near the Lehigh Navigation System.

Judith walked around the side of the bed and placed both hands on the thick mattress. Giving it a couple of firm pushes, she soon discovered it was soft and bouncy.

"Nothing like the thin straw mattress I used to sleep on as a child," she murmured. Nor did it compare to the hard bed she had shared with young Ellie Miller, the storekeeper's daughter, when she'd taken her first teaching position in northern New York.

Judith took a seat on the bed. She was pleased that during her stay here in Parryville she would room with the Reverend and Mrs. Jacobs and their twin daughters, Melissa and Melody, who were ten years old. The girls' bedroom was on the same floor as Judith's, and she could hear their laughter floating across the hall.

Starting Monday morning, I'll be Melissa and Melody's new teacher, she mused. *I pray things will go well.*

With a feeling of contentment, Judith gazed around the small, cozy room, noticing the blue and beige braided throw rug in the center of the floor, the oak dressing table and looking glass positioned along the far wall, and the colorful patchwork quilt spread across the bed. Then she stood and moved to the window, pushing the curtain aside so she could view the street below.

A little boy with shaggy brown hair and tattered overalls ran up and down the walkway in front of the parsonage. It was a blustery day, yet he wore no coat or hat. Judith noticed the slingshot hanging from his back pocket and a scruffy-looking dog nipping at his heels.

Will that child be in my classroom on Monday morning? Will he and the other children be agreeable and easy to teach, or will many be full of mischief, the way my brother Seth used to be?

She let the curtain fall into place and meandered across the room to check her appearance in the mirror. A lock of curly blond hair had come loose from the bun she wore at the back of her head, and she reached up to tuck it in place. Her cheeks looked pale, probably because she was tired from her train trip that morning, so she pinched them until they turned pink.

Judith tipped her head to one side as she studied her reflection. *Sorry to say, but there is nothing I can do to make my eyes look any better.*

From the time she was a little girl, Judith had been teased about having one brown eye and one blue. That and the fact that she was taller than most girls her age had made Judith believe she was unattractive, and nothing had happened during her twenty-six years to change her opinion of herself.

"Judith the odd one. Judith with the creepy eyes." She'd been called so many names when she was growing up.

Children can be cruel, she thought ruefully. *And that is one thing I won't tolerate in my classroom. No teasing or making fun of someone because they're different or don't have as many nice things as someone else.*

She returned to her seat on the bed. There was no point thinking negative thoughts or expecting trouble. No point feeling sorry for herself because she was an old maid who in all likelihood would never fall in love or get married.

"Who would want a tall woman with eyes that don't match?" she muttered. "No one ever has before." Besides, as a child of God who had confessed her sins and accepted Christ as her Savior, she knew that her heavenly Father cared for her just as she was—no matter what she or others might think of her appearance.

A knock on the bedroom door startled Judith. "Yes?"

"Supper's ready, Miss King," one of the twins announced.

"Mama said we should let you know," the other twin said.

Judith stood and smoothed the wrinkles in her long gray traveling dress. She had planned to change into something more presentable before joining the family for the evening meal, but there wasn't time now. "Tell your mother I'll be right there."

Judith heard the shuffle of the girls' feet as they headed down the hall, then the louder *clomp, clomp, clomp* as they descended the steps.

She drew in a deep breath and sent up a quick prayer. *Help me to fit in here, Lord, and bless the Jacobs family for offering me such a fine room.*

Ernie Snyder cupped his hands around his mouth and leaned over the bow of his boat. "Keep them mules movin' at a steady pace!" he called to his ten-year-old son, Andy.

The boy seemed determined to dawdle, as he clomped along the muddy towpath, like they had all the time in the world. "The mules don't like the mud puddles, and I can't make 'em go any faster!" he hollered back.

"We'll never get to Mauch Chunk at the rate we're goin'!" Ernie shouted into the wind. "Give Barney a thump on the rump if he won't move along!"

Andy did as he was told, and soon Barney, the lead mule, picked up speed. Clyde, the other mule, followed suit, and

Ernie breathed a sigh of relief. Maybe they wouldn't be late to pick up their load of coal after all.

"Keep us movin' without too many interruptions, Lord," Ernie prayed, glancing at the overcast sky. They'd had several days of rain, which had not only caused some flooding of the canal waters but had made the towpath almost impassable in several places. Even though it wasn't raining today and the waters had receded enough to travel, the towpath was a muddy mess, full of large puddles the mules refused to walk through. This took more time, as Andy and other mule drivers had to lead the stubborn critters around the standing water.

Soon winter would be here, and then much of the canal would be drained. Ernie planned to return with his two children to their small home outside of Parryville. He would spend the next few months cutting ice from the frozen sections of canal that had not been emptied.

"Papa, Sarah's lonely and needs a friend. Can we buy another dolly when we stop at the next store?"

Ernie glanced over his shoulder. His seven-year-old daughter, Grace, sat at the wooden table in the middle of the boat, which was where they ate most of their meals. The cornhusk doll she played with had been a gift from Ernie for her last birthday. Grace's long brown hair was unbraided today and lay across her slender shoulders in a mass of curls.

Ernie knew his daughter would need to go to school when they quit boating for the winter. It would be her first year at the one-room schoolhouse in Parryville, and he hoped she would do okay. Andy would go, too, even though the boy thought he didn't need any more schooling.

"Papa, are ya listenin' to me?" Grace asked in a whiny voice.

"I'm afraid you'll hafta be your doll's friend," Ernie replied. "Papa don't have enough money to buy another doll just now."

Grace's lower lip protruded, but Ernie knew he couldn't let her sway him. Money was tight, and unless he did well on his next couple of loads, he might have to let his helper go.

" 'Course that would mean I'd be stuck with all the cookin' and cleanin', not to mention havin' to steer the boat," he grumbled. No, he would scrimp by without luxuries in order to keep Jeb Walker as his helper, even if the elderly man was a complainer who sometimes fell asleep when he should be working. After Ernie's wife died of pneumonia, it hadn't been easy to find someone willing to watch Grace and do the cooking. Ernie was relieved when Jeb came to work for him shortly after Anna's death.

It's either keep Jeb on or get married again, Ernie told himself. *And who would want to marry an uneducated canal-boat captain like me?*

CHAPTER 2

As Judith stood behind her scarred wooden desk, she was surprised to see how few students were in class on this first day of school. Pastor Jacobs had said there would be more once the canal was closed for the winter, but in the meantime, there were only ten children in attendance.

Melissa and Melody, both in the third grade, shared a desk. Carl, the boy with the tattered overalls she'd seen from her bedroom window the other day, was in the second grade and sat beside Eric, another second grader. The other two boys, Garth and Roger, were fourth graders but looked much older. Judith wondered how many times they might have repeated the same grade. The four other girls in class were Beth, Sarah, Karen, and Ruby. Beth, the oldest, was in sixth grade; Karen and Sarah were fifth graders; and Ruby, the youngest, was in the first grade.

Besides the lack of students, Judith noted a deficiency of school supplies. Only a few pieces of chalk sat near the blackboard, and she didn't have nearly enough reading books to go around. Each child had been required to bring his or her own pencil and tablet. One map with several tears hung on the back wall. No art supplies were available, and the school's only bell was the small handheld one that sat on Judith's desk.

I'll need to make a trip to the general store after school lets out today, Judith mentally noted. *Maybe they'll have some of the things I need. If not, I'll speak to the school board and see if they would be willing to order a few items.*

Not that she wasn't used to going without. Her parents had never been well-off, and after Mama died giving birth to Judith's youngest brother, Papa became despondent and had a hard time holding on to a job. Just a few months after Mama's passing, he'd married Helen Smithers. Even though Papa's attitude had improved, Helen was stern, and she and Judith often clashed. At the age of eighteen, Judith had been offered a teaching position at a one-room schoolhouse several towns away, and she had eagerly accepted.

Judith turned her attention to the children, who sat at their desks, looking at her with expectant expressions. "The first thing I'd like you to do is write a one-page theme about yourself." She smiled. "That way I can get to know each of you better."

Melody's hand shot up.

"Yes?"

"What kinds of things do you want to know?"

"Yeah, this is gonna be hard," Eric put in. "Our old teacher never asked us to write anything about ourselves."

"Each teacher has her own way of doing things," Judith said patiently.

"How come you get to know us and we don't get to know you?" Carl spoke up.

"That's a fair question, so I'll tell you a few things about myself." Judith went to the blackboard and picked up a piece of chalk. She quickly wrote the following list:

> My name is Miss Judith King.
>
> I like to teach school.
>
> My favorite time of the year is fall, when the air is crisp and clean.
>
> The color I like best is blue.
>
> My favorite food is apple pie.

She turned to face the class. "Does that help?"

Carl wrinkled his nose. "Not really. We only know what you like."

"That's right," Sarah put in. "Tell us about yourself."

"What would you like to know?"

"Do you have any sisters or brothers?" Ruby asked.

Judith nodded. "I have two older brothers, one younger brother, and two half sisters."

"What's a half sister?" Melissa wanted to know.

"We both have the same father but different mothers."

"How can that be?" This question came from Garth.

None of the children raised their hands or waited to be called on, but Judith figured since this was the first day of school and everyone probably felt nervous, it would be all right to dispense with the usual rule.

She explained how her mother had died and her father remarried. Then later, his new wife had given birth to the two girls.

Carl leaned forward, his elbows on the desk and his chin cupped in his hands. "Have you always had those strange lookin' eyes?"

Judith squinted and rubbed the bridge of her nose, feeling like a headache might be forthcoming. How could the first assignment of the day have turned into questions and answers about her personal life? The last thing she wanted to discuss was the one physical feature she disliked the most about herself.

"One's blue and one's brown," Melody announced. "I've never known anyone with two different-colored eyes before."

Judith knew her cheeks must be red, for they felt like they were on fire. "My eyes have been like this since I was born."

"Do you see different colors out of each eye?" Carl questioned.

"No. I see everything the same as you do. Now would you please write something on your tablets about yourself?"

She sank onto the wooden chair behind her desk. This was going to be a lengthy first day of school!

"Hey, boss, can we stop at Henson's General Store!" Jeb called to Ernie from the stern of the boat.

"What are ya needin'?" Ernie hollered back.

"Just a couple of kitchen supplies!"

"Can't it wait? I'm tryin' to keep on schedule!"

"Shouldn't take that long to get a few things!"

Ernie released an exasperated groan and signaled Andy to slow the mules. "We're stoppin' at the store!" he shouted.

Andy waved, and soon he had the towrope tied to a tree near the edge of the canal, not far from the general store.

Ernie lowered the gangplank, and Jeb ambled off like he had all the time in the world.

"Can we get some candy, Papa?" Grace asked, leaning over the railing and swishing her long braids from side to side. Apparently Jeb had taken the time to do her hair up properly this morning. Ernie noticed she was even dressed in a pair of clean overalls.

He gave one of her braids a gentle tug. "You think I have money to spend on candy, little one?"

"Just one hunk of licorice will do."

He chuckled and hoisted her onto his shoulders. "Well, okay. We'll go inside the store and see what's in the candy counter."

Ernie was pleased to see that Andy had already tied up the mules, and he patted the boy on top of his head. "Why don't ya run into the store and see if you can find somethin' to satisfy your sweet tooth?"

When Andy looked up, his dark eyes gleamed and his lips curved into a smile. "Ya mean it, Papa?"

"Said so, didn't I?"

The boy didn't have to be asked twice. He galloped off toward the store, and by the time Ernie and Grace entered the building, Andy already had an all-day sucker in his hand.

Ernie set Grace on the floor in front of the candy counter and went to join Jeb and Lon Henson at the back of the building.

"Got any chewin' tobacco?" Jeb asked the store owner.

Before Lon could reply, Ernie stepped between the two men. "Jeb don't need none of that awful stuff. It stains your teeth, makes your breath smell foul, and it's bad for your health."

Jeb ran a hand along the bald spot on top of his head. "Where'd ya hear that, boss?"

Ernie wasn't sure where he'd heard it, but he wasn't about to let on. Instead, he merely shrugged and said, "Take my word for it, Jeb."

"Yeah, well, I like chewin' tobacco," his helper argued. "Gives me somethin' to do with my mouth." He squinted at Ernie. "But then, I don't know nothin'—just ask anybody."

Lon shook his graying head and pounded Jeb on the back. "Ya know plenty 'bout flappin' your gums!"

Jeb looked like he was ready to offer another comeback, but the front door opened, and a blast of chilly air whipped into the store.

"Whew! Sure is gettin' cold out," Lon said, rubbing his shirtsleeves and turning toward the front of the building.

"Yep. Won't be long now, and the canal will be shut down till spring," Ernie agreed. He glanced in the direction Lon was heading and froze. A young woman stood near the front counter talking to Grace. She was tall, with blond hair pulled back into a bun, and curly bangs spreading across her forehead. She wore a solid navy-blue dress that touched the top of her black leather shoes, and a white knitted shawl was draped around her shoulders.

"Now there's a looker for ya," Jeb said with a crooked grin. "Don't recollect seein' that beauty 'round here before, have you, boss?"

Ernie shook his head, unable to form the right words. He stared at the woman a few seconds, then pulled his gaze away. This wasn't right. She could be married, and if she was, he had no call to be gawking at her.

Don't have no reason to be starin' even if she ain't married, he berated himself. *The only thing I should be thinkin' about is gettin' my load of coal hauled up to Easton.*

"Ain't ya gonna go up front and see why that woman's talkin' to Grace?" Jeb's bony elbow connected with Ernie's ribs, and he jumped.

"Hey, cut that out!"

"I was only tryin' to get your attention. You've been standin' there like you was struck dumb or somethin'."

Ernie ran a hand through his thick, wavy hair and grimaced. "You're right. I should find out who she is and why she's talkin' to my daughter."

Before Jeb had a chance to comment, Ernie tromped across the wooden floor and stopped beside the blond-haired woman. He cleared his throat. "Ahem."

She turned and offered him a tentative smile, then glanced down at his daughter. "Is this your papa, Grace?"

The child nodded and pointed to the woman. "This here's Miss Judith King, Papa. She's the new schoolteacher in Parryville. She says she ain't married and don't got no kids."

"But I do like children, and that's why I teach." Judith extended her hand. "It's nice to meet you, Mr.—"

"Snyder. Ernie Snyder." He shook the woman's hand and then released it, feeling like an awkward schoolboy who didn't know up from down.

"Your daughter tells me she's never been to school before."

"That's right, but as soon as the canal's drained, she'll be goin' with her brother." Ernie motioned to Andy, who stood near the potbellied stove warming his hands as he held the sucker between his lips.

"That's good to know, but don't you think your children should be in school all year?" Judith questioned.

Ernie's defenses rose, and he clenched his fingers while holding his hands at his sides. "I own my own boat, and my kids need to be with me when the canal's up and runnin'."

"What about your wife? Can't she bring the children to school?"

His forehead wrinkled. "Anna's dead. Died a few years ago from pneumonia."

Judith blinked a couple of times, and he noticed that one of her eyes was blue and the other was brown. He'd never seen anyone with two different-colored eyes before, and it was hard not to stare.

"I'm sorry about your wife, Mr. Snyder," she said in a sincere tone. "I'm sure you're doing the best you can by your children."

"Yep, he sure is. That's why he hired me to cook, clean, and watch out for Grace," Jeb declared. He stepped up beside Ernie and offered Judith a toothless grin.

"My kids don't get the kind of learnin' that some do," Ernie said, "but I've taught 'em a few Bible verses, and they can recite several by heart."

"That's right," Grace chimed in. " 'God has made everything beautiful in his time.' Ecclesiastes 3:11."

Judith touched the child on the shoulder. "Well done."

"I know more. Want to hear 'em?"

Before the schoolteacher had a chance to reply, Ernie tapped Grace on the shoulder and said, "Not now, daughter. We need to pay for our things and get back to the boat."

Judith leaned over so she was eye level with Grace. "I'd be happy to hear some other verses when you come to school." She straightened again and looked directly at Ernie. "I'll look forward to having your children in class. . .sometime next month?"

"Right. The weather's gettin' colder now, so most of the canal will probably be drained by then." *She's tall. Really tall.* Ernie chewed on that thought a few seconds. *Never met a woman who could look me right in the eye.*

He shook his head, hoping the action would get him thinking straight. Then, with a sudden need for some fresh air, he slapped some money on the counter in front of the storekeeper. "Give Jeb the change when he finishes his business."

"Will do," Lon said with a nod.

Ernie grabbed his daughter's hand. "Me and Grace will be waitin' on the boat, Jeb."

"Okay, boss. Andy and me will be along just as soon as we gather up the supplies."

Remembering what his mama used to say about good manners, Ernie called over his shoulder, "Nice meetin' ya, Miss King!" Then he and Grace went out the door.

CHAPTER 3

As Judith stood on the front porch of the schoolhouse, ringing her bell, she was pleased to see the Snyder children tromping up the path with their father. School had been in session a little over a month, and now that freezing weather was upon them, many of the canalers' children would be coming to the new schoolteacher for some book learning.

"Good morning, Mr. Snyder," she said as Ernie and his children stepped onto the porch.

He gave his navy-blue stocking cap a quick tug and offered her a crooked grin. "Aw, just call me Ernie. 'Mr. Snyder' sounds too formal-like."

Judith smiled in return. "Ernie it is, then." She glanced at his daughter, noting several places where her jacket was torn.

"Hello, Grace. I've been looking forward to having you in my class."

Grace stared at her rubber boots. " 'Mornin', Miss King."

Ernie gave his daughter's arm a pat. "She's feelin' kind of nervous, what with this bein' her first day of school and all."

Judith's heart went out to the child. When she was a girl, she had been shy and self-conscious, rarely speaking unless she was spoken to and always worried about her appearance.

"You'll be fine once you get to know everyone," Judith assured the child. She bent down, so she was eye level with Ernie's son. "And what's your name?"

"Andy," the boy mumbled. "Papa said I have to come to school, but I'd rather be helpin' him cut ice all winter."

Judith glanced back at Ernie. "You're an ice cutter?"

He nodded. "Just durin' the winter months. Gotta make a livin' somehow when I can't run the boat."

"Do you live on the boat all year?" she asked.

"Naw. We have a little house on the far side of town. Like to hunker down there durin' the colder months."

When Judith was about to comment, she heard a ruckus going on in the schoolhouse, and her attention was drawn inside. "Please come in and take off your coats," she said, motioning to the door. "Apparently I've got some rowdy students who must be anxious for their day to begin."

As they stepped inside the schoolhouse, a wadded-up piece of paper sailed across the room, just missing Judith's head. She hadn't seen who had thrown it, but from the guilty look on Roger's face, she suspected it was him.

She bent to pick up the paper. "Everyone, please take your seats. We have two new students today—Andy and Grace Snyder."

Ernie shuffled his feet a few times. "I reckon I should be headin' back to work. I'll be by after school to pick up my kids." He looked first at Andy, then at Grace. "You two behave yourselves, ya hear?"

"Yes, Papa," Grace said meekly.

Andy only gave a brief nod.

Judith motioned to an empty desk near the front of the room. "Why don't the two of you sit there today?"

As the Snyder children took their seats, she escorted Ernie to the door. "I'm sure they'll be fine, Mr. Snyder—I mean, Ernie."

He grunted and reached up to rub his chin, which appeared to have recently been shaved. Judging from the spot of dried blood, Judith figured he'd probably nicked himself.

With a quick "See ya later," Ernie tromped out the door.

That man needs a warmer coat, Judith thought when she noticed Ernie pull the collar of his threadbare jacket around his neck. *And what a nice father for escorting his children to school.*

As Ernie headed for the icehouse on the other side of town, all he could think about was Judith King, with her haunting multicolored eyes and dimpled smile. It was dumb, just plain stupid, to think a woman as beautiful and smart as she was would ever give anyone like him a second glance.

I only went through the fourth grade. If she knew that, she'd probably think I was a poor canaler who's dumber than dirt. Ernie kicked a hefty stone with the toe of his boot, hoping the action would get him thinking about something else.

"Sure hope my boy don't give the teacher no sass," he mumbled, shoving his hands into his jacket pockets. Andy had been a handful since Anna died, often playing tricks on his sister and not always minding the mules the way he should. Ernie knew if he didn't stay firm with the child, he might grow up to be lazy.

Ernie had begun walking the mules when he was eight years old. Later, when his pa was sure he could handle the boat, he'd become the spotter and sometimes got to steer. From the beginning Ernie had known he would own a canal boat someday. He loved being on the water, moving up and down the canal hauling anthracite coal, and he hoped Andy would want to follow in his footsteps—although with the growing competition from trains, the family business might come to an end before then.

Ernie picked up his pace. His primary goal in life was to see that his kids were properly cared for. He also knew it was important for them to memorize some Bible verses and learn to do an honest day's work.

Guess they might need a bit more book learnin' than I had, too.

Judith stood at the window overlooking the schoolyard, watching the children during their afternoon recess. Even though it was cold outside, it was good for them to run and play. When the students came back inside, they would be ready to settle down. She might have a spelling bee for the older ones and get the younger children involved in an art project. Soon Christmas would be here, and some colorful decorations for the schoolhouse would be a nice addition.

Judith turned to study the room. *I'll need to think about a Christmas program soon and who will get what parts. The children would probably enjoy singing some Christmas carols, too.*

A commotion outside drew Judith's attention back to the window. Several children stood in a circle, chanting, "Hit him! Hit him! Hit him!"

Judith rushed out the door, not bothering to fetch her shawl. "What's going on?" she shouted above the noise.

The chanting stopped, but no one spoke. Then she spotted Grace crouched next to the teeter-totter.

When Judith pushed through the circle, she realized that Andy stood in the center, toe-to-toe with Garth. Both boys held up their fists as though ready to take a swing.

She ducked between them. "What is the problem?"

Garth squinted his eyes, and Andy stared at the ground.

Judith rubbed her hands briskly over her arms as the stinging cold penetrated her skin. "If someone doesn't tell me what happened, the whole class will be punished."

Sarah stepped forward. "Garth was makin' fun of Andy's sister, calling her 'sissy face' and 'runt.' So Andy challenged him to a fight, but you got here before either could land the first punch."

"Is it true that you were calling Grace names?" Judith asked, taking Garth by the shoulders and turning him to face her.

He shrugged. "Maybe."

Judith's patience was growing thin, and she prayed for wisdom. "Either you did or you didn't. Which is it?"

Garth lifted his chin and glared at her. "Okay, I did, but the little baby deserved it."

"No one deserves to be called names," Judith said sternly. She remembered some of the names she had been called as a child. *Giraffe with the long neck. Judith the freak. The girl with the spooky eyes.*

"Garth, you will stay after school today, and we'll talk about your punishment then." She tapped him on the shoulder. "In the meantime, I want you to tell Andy and Grace you're sorry for being rude."

The boy folded his arms in an unyielding pose. "Why should I apologize? He's the one who said he was gonna clean my clock for teasin' his baby sister."

Garth had a point. Andy shouldn't have started the fight. However, Judith figured he was only defending his sister. "Andy, apologize to Garth, and Garth, you do the same. Then you must tell Grace you're sorry."

With an exaggerated huff, Andy wrinkled his nose and mumbled, "Sorry."

Garth followed suit.

Judith shooed the others inside, then took Garth's arm and led him across the schoolyard to the teeter-totters where Grace was still squatted.

"Sorry for callin' ya sissy face and runt," the boy said, his jaw tight.

"Let's get back to class." Judith reached for Grace's hand, but the little girl stayed firmly in place. Garth had already sprinted toward the schoolhouse.

"Come on, sweetheart," Judith pleaded. "You can't stay out here—it's too cold."

"I want my papa."

"He said he would return after school."

"I wanna go home."

"You can't go home until school is over for the day."

The child gave no response, and Judith, though shivering from the cold, knelt beside her. "I remember when I saw you at the general store last month," she said. "You had licorice candy."

Grace nodded.

"Would you come inside if I promise to give you a piece of licorice when school lets out?"

"You got some?"

"Yes, in my desk. I keep it there for children who've done well on their assignments or have been extra good."

"I didn't do nothin' good," Grace said, her chin quivering.

"Obeying the teacher is a good thing. So if you come with me now, your reward will be the licorice."

The child clambered to her feet. "Okay."

Judith breathed a sigh of relief. The role of a schoolteacher brought lots of challenges, and there were days like today when she wondered if she was up to them.

CHAPTER 4

The days sped by quickly as Judith settled in with her larger class. Five more children from the canal had started coming to school, so now there were seventeen. Grace wasn't quite as shy as she had been at first, and Andy and Garth had calmed down, too.

Even though all the children behaved better in class and during recess, Judith felt some concern because of their lack of interaction. She had tried a question-and-answer time following their lessons, but most of the children just sat there, staring at their desk or out the window.

Today Judith decided to try something new—something she hoped everyone would take part in.

"Children," she said, clapping her hands together. "I've

come up with an idea I shall call the letter box."

She reached under her desk and retrieved the small cardboard box she'd put there before class, placing it in the middle of her desk. "During our art lesson today, we'll decorate this and put a hole in the lid. Then each of you may write down any questions, ideas, or concerns you have and put it in the box. If your letter is signed, you will receive a letter back. If it's not, I will respond to it orally in front of the class."

Ruby's hand shot up.

"Yes?"

The freckle-faced little girl grinned. "I'd like to get a letter from you, Teacher."

"Thank you, Ruby."

"Me, too," several of the girls chorused.

Noisy snickers from the back of the room drew Judith's attention to the boys who sat in the last row of desks. "Would one of you care to tell me what you think is so funny?"

"Nothin', Miss King." Roger folded his hands in front of him and sat as straight as a ruler.

"What about you, Eric?" Judith questioned. "Why were you laughing?"

The boy slunk down in his seat, and Carl, who sat beside Eric, jabbed him in the ribs.

"Hey, cut that out! Want me to slug you?"

Maybe this wasn't such a good idea, Judith thought with dismay. *If the children don't take this project seriously, nothing will be gained by doing it.*

"I like the idea of a letter box," Andy spoke up.

"Why is that?" Judith asked.

The boy pulled his fingers through the shaggy brown hair curling around his ears. "Seems like a fun way to learn about others, that's all."

Judith nodded, feeling more hopeful.

"Can we decorate the box now?" Karen asked.

"I suppose we could."

"Yes!" the children shouted.

"After I hand out some glue, scissors, and paper, you can all get busy," Judith said. "If you each make a small decoration, we'll take turns gluing them to the box."

The room became quiet, as every child began work on their decorations. A short time later, the plain cardboard box had been transformed into a collage of brightly colored squares, circles, and triangles. Judith printed the words Letter Box on a piece of white paper and glued it to the center of the box. She allowed Beth, the oldest girl, to cut a hole in the top, and the box was placed on Judith's desk.

"For the next half hour, you may each write your questions or comments on a slip of paper. When I ring the bell for recess, you can deposit them in the box," Judith announced. "A few minutes before it's time to go home, I'll read some of the letters that are unsigned and hand out my reply to those who have included their name."

"I hope Teacher reads mine," she overheard Ruby whisper to Grace.

Grace only nodded in reply, as she seemed to be concentrating on the paper before her.

Judith drew in a deep breath and returned to her desk. *This project might be the very thing that will make my class successful.*

Ernie shivered as he clomped through the fresh-fallen snow, on his way to the small building where the ice he'd been cutting would be stored. It was early December, and the weather had turned bitterly cold. He hated to think what the rest of winter might be like.

"Probably need to get me a heavier coat and a new pair of gloves," he muttered, glancing at the gaping hole in the thumb of his left glove. "Sure hate to spend money on clothes for me, though. Not when there are so many other needs."

Ernie's children came first, and they always had. That was why he worked such long hours hauling coal during the warmer months, and it was why he also planned to work hard this winter, cutting ice. If anyone needed a new coat, it was Grace, and he hoped to get her one for Christmas. Andy needed a new pair of boots, too. The ones he wore now were pinching his toes.

Ernie thought about his helper and wondered if Jeb had been able to find work in Easton. Jeb had a daughter who lived there, and he would stay with her, even if he didn't secure a job for the winter.

The thought had crossed Ernie's mind to look for work in the city, but his home was in Parryville, and he hated to uproot Andy and Grace. They were happy here. Happy with their new schoolteacher, too.

A vision of Judith King flashed into Ernie's mind. Several times he'd gone to pick up his kids after school, yet he'd never said more than "Howdy, how are you?" or "Hope my kids are doin' okay" to the schoolmarm. He'd wanted to say more. Truth was Ernie would have liked to invite Judith to join him and the kids for supper at Baker's Café, but he couldn't work up the nerve.

"Not that she'd give me a second look," he mumbled. "She's probably had all kinds of offers from men a lot smarter and handsomer than me."

Ernie was glad when the icehouse came into view. He was supposed to meet Abe McGinnis there, and the two of them would spend most of the day cutting ice on a section of canal nearby that hadn't been drained. Ernie figured hard work was good. It kept him too busy to do much thinking, and when he worked up a sweat, he didn't mind the cold so much.

"Yep. That's what I need all right," Ernie mumbled, opening the door of the icehouse. "Need to get busy and quit thinkin' about that purty schoolteacher."

While the children romped in the snow during recess, Judith sat at her desk, reading the letters that had been deposited in the letter box a short time ago. The first one was from Bobby Collins, and it read:

Dear Teacher:

How come you have two different-colored eyes?

The boy was new to class and was one of those who led the mules along the canal. Judith knew he hadn't been at school the day she'd explained to the students about her unusual eyes. Therefore, he deserved an answer to his question.

Dear Bobby:

God makes each person different, and He chose to give me one brown eye and one blue.

Miss King

She unfolded the next piece of paper.

Dear Teacher:

How do I get to be a teacher like you?

Ruby Miller

Judith's reply was:

Dear Ruby:

Study hard, get good grades, and someday you might be offered the job of teaching school, too.

Miss King

The next letter caused Judith to do some serious thinking.

Dear Teacher:

Why can't we have a longer recess?

Carl Higgins

Judith tapped her pencil along the edge of her desk. Carl's question was one she had asked herself when she was a girl. Maybe she could extend their recess a bit, perhaps on Friday afternoons.

The next letter was a surprise.

Dear Teacher:

I wish you was my mama. I think Papa might like that, too.

The letter was unsigned.

Judith felt a trickle of perspiration roll down her forehead. If one of the children thought this way, could there be more with the same idea? And who had written this note?

She studied the handwriting, noting that the letters were uneven and some were barely more than a scribble. It had to be written by one of the younger children.

Could it be Carl? she wondered. He seemed to like Judith and often gave her a hug when no one was looking.

Judith heard the children's footsteps clomping across the porch. "How can I possibly answer this letter out loud?" she moaned.

Chapter 5

As Judith left the pastor's home and headed toward the church on Sunday morning, she noticed several of her students coming up the walkway. Grace and Andy were not among them, however, and neither was their father.

When Ernie mentioned that he had taught his children some memory verses, Judith assumed he was a churchgoing man. Apparently she'd been wrong, for in the month he'd been living in Parryville, she had not seen him at church even once.

" 'Mornin', Miss King!" Beth called with a cheery wave.

Judith nodded at her student and smiled. Already she had a fondness for those she taught, and she truly liked living and working in this small town near the canal. Reverend and Mrs. Jacobs had made her feel right at home, although their identical twin daughters could be a little trying at times. On more than one occasion, Melody and Melissa had attempted to fool their teacher by taking on the other sister's identity, but Judith had finally figured out who was who.

She continued walking toward the church, as she thought about the past week and how the atmosphere in the classroom had changed since they had begun using the letter box. The children seemed more attentive, and they were getting to know one another better.

Judith reflected on the way she had handled the unsigned letter from the child who wished Teacher could be his or her mama. She'd waited until the end of the day to respond to the letters that weren't signed. Since there was only enough time left to read a couple, the personal one about her was left unread.

The following day, Judith had made a new rule. "Starting today, I will answer all letters addressed to me, even if they aren't signed. My replies will be written and put inside another box, and I'll set both boxes on a shelf inside the coatroom. If you write an unsigned letter and want an answer, you may look for it in the reply box."

In response to the letter about her being someone's mama, Judith had written:

Dear Student:

It's nice to know you would like me to be your mother.

Even though that's not possible, I care about you and everyone in my class.

Miss King

Judith pulled her thoughts aside, as she climbed the steps and entered the church. Reverend Jacobs was inside the foyer, and he greeted her with a smile. "May I speak with you a moment, Judith?"

"Of course." She followed the pastor to the other side of the room, where they could talk in private.

"I've just learned that Margaret Jones fell on the ice and broke her leg last night," he said.

Judith frowned. "I'm sorry to hear that."

"Margaret has been teaching our girls' Sunday school class for the past year, but she'll have to give up teaching for a while." He tugged on the end of his dark mustache. "I was wondering if you might consider taking over for her."

Judith didn't hesitate. "I'd be happy to, although I'm not prepared with anything today."

"Could you read them a story from the Bible and have them draw a picture of what they've learned?"

Judith didn't want to leave any little girl without a Sunday school teacher, so she agreeably nodded.

"Thank you. I appreciate that." Reverend Jacobs pointed down the hall. "The girls meet in the last room on the left."

Judith was prepared to head in that direction when she noticed Ernie and his children enter the building. Her heart pounded as their gazes met. What was there about the man that fascinated her so? They were as different as her unmatched eyes. She was a schoolteacher who carefully chose her words—Ernie worked the canal and often spoke in broken sentences. She was tall and unattractive—he was ruggedly handsome and strong. Yet Ernie's apparent love for his children and his friendly smile had touched Judith's heart from the moment they had first met.

"Good morning. How are you, Ernie?" Judith asked when he and his children came alongside her.

"Fair to middlin'." He stared down at his boots. "Are my kids doin' okay in school?"

She glanced at his children and smiled. "I believe they are."

"I like the letter box, Teacher," Grace said.

"I'm glad." Judith tapped Andy on the shoulder. "How about you? Do you still think our letter box is a good idea?"

He shrugged. "Did at first, but some of the kids write sissy stuff."

"Letter box?" Ernie tipped his head and gave Judith a curious look.

She quickly explained what the box was and how it worked.

Ernie rubbed his chin, which Judith noticed had again been recently shaved. Only this time there were no nicks or bloody scabs.

"Hmm. . .might be a good idea," he mumbled.

She nodded. "I believe some of the children have been able to say things they might not have had the courage to say in person."

"I wrote a letter once, but I didn't sign—" Grace's cheeks

turned bright red, and she covered her mouth with the back of her hand.

Judith didn't wish to cause the child further embarrassment, so she reached for Grace's hand. "Starting today, I'll be teaching the girls' Sunday school class, so if you'd like to come along, we can go there now."

"How 'bout me and the boy?" Ernie motioned to Andy, who stood off to one side fidgeting with the stocking cap he held in his hands.

"I believe Deacon Miller teaches the class for the boys, which is somewhere down the hall. I can help Andy find it when Grace and I go to our class." She nodded toward the sanctuary. "Reverend Jacobs meets with the men in there, while Mrs. Jacobs teaches the women in another classroom."

Ernie opened his mouth, like he might want to say something more, but he shrugged and headed for the sanctuary instead.

Judith led the way down the hall, with Andy and Grace at her side.

Ernie took a seat on a pew in the back row, feeling self-conscious and as out of place as a snowball in summer. He hadn't been in Sunday school for many years. He had brought his children to church several times, although it was mostly during the winter months when they lived in town. He knew it was time for the kids to get regular Bible learning, and he figured they would receive a lot more in Sunday school than what he could teach them at home.

Ernie glanced at his faded blue trousers. They were the only pair he had that didn't have holes or a noticeable stain. The white shirt he wore had fit him at one time, but after many washings in too hot of water, it had shrunk. The cuffs were now several inches above his wrists.

"It's good to see you this morning," Reverend Jacobs said, tapping him on the shoulder. "Wouldn't you like to move up closer so you can hear the lesson better?"

Ernie noticed that all the other men had taken seats in the first two rows. Reluctantly he stood and followed the pastor up front, easing himself onto a third-row pew and trying not to look conspicuous.

Sure hope the preacher don't ask me no questions, he thought with a frown. *I read a few Bible verses every day and have memorized some, but when it comes to speakin' out loud, I'd sound like a dimwit.*

"Our lesson today will be from Proverbs," the pastor announced. "So if you will open your Bibles to chapter 16, we'll take turns reading."

A trickle of sweat rolled down Ernie's forehead, as he heard the rustle of pages. *Maybe he won't call on me. And if he does, I'll just say I left my Bible at home, which won't be a lie.*

"In this passage of scripture, one verse I'd like to bring out has to do with the way we talk," Reverend Jacobs said. "Henry Bonner, would you read verse 24?"

Henry, a tall, heavyset bank teller, stood and cleared his throat real loud.

" 'Pleasant words are as an honeycomb, sweet to the soul, and health to the bones.' "

"Now if the kind words we speak are pleasant enough to be health to our bones, what might our unkind words be compared to?" The preacher's gaze traveled from one man to the other.

Ernie knew the answer to that, but he wasn't about to raise his hand.

"Let's turn back to chapter 15." Reverend Jacobs nodded at Frank Gookins, who Ernie knew was also a canaler. "Would you read verse 1?"

Ernie held his breath, waiting to see what Frank would do. The man was as uneducated as Ernie. Surely he would refuse to read out loud.

Frank stood, and in a faltering voice he said, " 'A soft. . . uh. . .answer turn-eth a-way wrath: but grieve. . .uh. . . grieve. . .' "

"Grievous," the pastor said patiently.

" 'But griev-ous words—stir up—anger.' " Frank closed the Bible and flopped onto the pew with a look of relief.

Reverend Jacobs smiled. "Thank you, Frank."

Ernie groaned inwardly. He felt sorry for poor Frank but was relieved it hadn't been him the pastor called on.

"This is what we've learned," Reverend Jacobs continued. "If our words are pleasant, they will be like honeycomb, bringing health to the bones. If our words are grievous, they will stir up anger."

Ernie thought about his helper. Jeb could cut a body down

with only a few words. It was a good thing the man wasn't in charge of the canal boat because there were times when more than one boat arrived at the lock gates. Ernie could only imagine how Jeb would handle things if he were the boss. He'd probably shake his fist at the other captain and holler, "Get your boat outta my way, or I'll box your ears!"

Ernie stared at his calloused hands. *I may not know lots of big words, but them that do come from my mouth oughta be kind. I'll need to keep prayin' for Jeb and try to set a good example.*

On Monday morning, Judith was surprised to see Ernie walk up to the schoolhouse with his children. She knew he'd been busy cutting ice, and lately Grace and Andy had come to school by themselves.

"Good morning, Ernie. Good morning, children," she said with a smile.

"Mornin'," they responded in unison.

The children scampered into the classroom, but their father lingered a few moments on the porch. "Is there something you want to say, Ernie?" Judith asked.

He jammed his hands into his jacket pocket and rocked back and forth on the heels of his boots. "Well, I. . .uh. . .was wonderin' if—"

Carl and Eric raced past just then, bumping into Ernie and knocking him against Judith.

"Oh!" she exclaimed, trying to regain her balance.

Ernie grabbed her around the waist. "Are. . .are you okay?"

The man's face was red like an apple, and Judith figured hers was, too. "I–I'm fine," she said breathlessly.

Ernie released his hold on her, and she took a step back. "Guess I'd best be goin'," he mumbled.

"But I thought you wanted to ask me something."

"It weren't nothin' important." He shook his head and hurried away.

Judith shivered, realizing how cold she'd become standing on the porch with no wrap. "I wish I knew what Ernie had planned to say," she murmured. "He certainly is a man of few words."

CHAPTER 6

While the children were outside during afternoon recess, Judith sat at her desk, reading the letters she had found in the letter box earlier. Two were unsigned, both asking questions about whom the teacher thought was her best student.

"Strange," Judith murmured. "Either the same person wrote both letters, or two students are competing for my attention."

She figured it was probably Melody and Melissa. The twins were competitive, and Judith had noticed several times at home the girls often argued and tried to get one of their parents to take a side.

Judith turned the notes over and wrote the same response on each one:

Dear Student:

I care about all the children in my class, and it wouldn't be right to have one favorite. Keep doing your best, and you will learn much.

Miss King

Loud voices in the schoolyard captured Judith's attention, and she set her pencil and paper aside. Opening the front door, she stepped onto the porch. Several of the boys raced around the yard shaking their fists and hollering at one another.

"He did it!"

"No, it was your fault."

"He started it."

"No way—it was you!"

A few of the girls leaned over the porch and pointed, like there might be someone or something beneath them.

"What happened?" Judith asked, easing her body between Melody and Karen.

"It's Andy Snyder," Melody replied. "Roger shoved him off the porch, and now the bully's bein' chased by some of the other boys who know what he did to Andy was wrong."

Judith's heart lurched when she saw Andy lying on the ground, whimpering and holding his right arm. She hurried down the steps and knelt to examine the boy. His arm was red and starting to swell, but it didn't look like it was out of place. "Andy, is it true that Roger pushed you?"

The child nodded, as tears rolled down his cheeks.

"Why did he do that?"

"Roger was shoutin' names at Andy and some of the other boys from the canal," Karen spoke up. "He said they were a bunch of dirty canalers who don't have no more brains than a dumb mule."

"That's right," Melody agreed. "I think Andy got sick of it, 'cause he told Roger what he thought. That's when the mean fellow pushed him off the porch."

Judith clenched her fingers. She hated name-calling and thought she had made it clear that it would not be tolerated. Glancing at Andy's arm again, she knew the first order of business was to take him to the doctor in case it was broken. She would deal with the troublemakers tomorrow morning.

"Clem, please get my horse hitched to the buggy," she called to one of the older boys. "When that's done, could you find Andy's father and let him know what's happened? Be sure to tell him that I'm taking his son to see the doctor."

"Sure, Miss King. I know right where Ernie's cuttin' ice today, 'cause my pa's workin' there, too." Clem sprinted toward the corral where Judith kept her horse during school hours.

"Beth, would you please take over for me until school is out?" Judith asked the older girl.

Beth's dark eyes became huge. "You—you want me to teach the students?"

Judith shook her head. "Just have them finish their reading assignment and then dismiss the class."

Beth nodded and called to the other children, while Judith helped Andy to his feet and over to her waiting buggy.

"Can I go along?" Grace asked, running beside them.

"Of course. Hurry and climb into the back of the buggy."

A short time later, Judith and Grace sat in the waiting area at the doctor's office, while Andy was being examined in the next room.

"What if my brother's arm is broken?" Grace questioned. "How's he gonna do his schoolwork?"

Judith patted Grace's hand, and in so doing, she noticed a tear in the sleeve of the child's faded green dress. "Would you like me to fix this for you?"

Grace nodded. "Jeb and Papa don't know how to sew. Mama used to fix the rips in my clothes, but now she's in heaven with Jesus. Papa said so." The child stared at her hands, clasped tightly in her lap.

Judith reached into her satchel and retrieved a needle and thread. As she stitched the tear, she told Grace about losing her own mother when she was ten years old.

"Guess maybe our mamas are visitin' each other up there with God." Grace's tone was so sincere—and her expression of such conviction—it caused tears to spring into Judith's eyes.

She sniffed and tried to keep her focus on the needle going back and forth through the hole in Grace's dress. "I'm wondering why you don't join the other girls at school whenever they play on the swings during recess," she asked, feeling the need to change the subject.

The child stared up at Judith with huge brown eyes and shrugged her slim shoulders.

"Don't they make you feel welcome?"

"They say mean things to me, 'cause Papa's a dirty old

canaler. Some even sing that awful song we don't like."

"What song is that?"

" 'You rusty ole canaler, you'll never get rich.' " Grace's eyebrows drew together. "That's all the words I can say, 'cause Papa says some of 'em are bad." Her chin came up and quivered slightly. "He said if he ever catches me or Andy sayin' bad words, he'll wash our mouths out with soap."

Judith nodded and broke off the piece of thread then tied a knot. "There, it's almost as good as new."

"Thank you, Teacher."

"You're welcome."

The front door opened then, and Ernie rushed into the room.

Grace jumped up and hurried to his side. "Papa!"

He patted the top of his daughter's head, but Judith could tell he was barely aware of the young girl's presence. "What happened? Where's my boy? Is he gonna be okay?" Ernie's eyes were wide, and his face was a mask of concern.

Judith stood and moved to stand beside him. She quickly explained how one of the boys had been calling names and then told what had followed.

Ernie's eyes flashed angrily. "I knew it was a mistake to put my kids in school with a bunch of young-uns who think they're better'n us." He leveled Judith with a look that made her toes curl inside her high-top shoes. "I can't believe you'd let somethin' like this happen."

She reached out and touched the man's arm, hoping to calm him down, but it seemed to have the opposite effect.

Ernie pulled away like he'd been stung by a hornet. Strangely enough, Judith felt as if some stinging insect had attacked her, too. Could it have been the contact of her fingers touching Ernie's skin?

She took a step back. "All children tend to argue and fuss at times. But you can be sure the boy who pushed Andy will be punished."

"Glad to hear it." Ernie looked around the room. "Where is my boy? Is he gonna be okay?"

"He's with Dr. Smith, and we should know something soon." Judith nodded toward the wooden chairs. "In the meantime, why don't we have a seat?"

With an exaggerated shrug, Ernie marched across the room and flopped into a chair. Grace took the seat beside him, and Judith sat on the other side.

"Teacher fixed the hole in my dress," Grace said, lifting her elbow and leaning toward her father.

His face softened, and he gave Judith a half smile. "That was right nice." Then he glanced back at his daughter. "Did ya tell your teacher thanks?"

"I did."

Just then the adjoining door opened, and Dr. Smith stepped out. Andy followed, his right arm in a sling.

Ernie jumped to his feet, as did Judith. They both took a step forward and, in so doing, collided. Judith's face heated with embarrassment, as Ernie's hand went around her waist. This was the second time today he'd kept her from falling over. "You all right?" he croaked.

Not trusting her voice, she only nodded.

Ernie turned to face the doctor. "How's my boy? Is his arm broke?"

Dr. Smith shook his head. "It's just a bad sprain, but he'll need to wear the sling until the swelling goes down."

"Glad you're not hurt real bad," Ernie said, patting Andy's shoulder.

Andy grimaced. "Me, too, but it still smarts somethin' awful."

"It'll feel better in a day or so." Ernie nodded toward the chairs where Grace sat. "Have a seat by your sister while I settle up with the doc."

Judith joined Grace and Andy, while Ernie and Dr. Smith tended to business.

"I'm sorry about your accident," she said to Andy. "You can be sure that Roger will be punished."

Andy hung his head. "He thinks I'm dumb and dirty 'cause I lead my papa's mules."

"You're not dumb, Andy. You're a quick learner, and—"

"It's time to go," Ernie announced, sauntering toward them. "Should we stop at the café for somethin' to eat before we go home?"

"Can Teacher come, too?" The question came from Grace as she grabbed hold of Judith's hand.

"I should probably get home," Judith was quick to say. She didn't want Ernie to feel obligated to include her in their supper plans.

Ernie shuffled his feet. "Would ya. . .uh. . .like to join us at the café? You're more'n welcome."

Her heartbeat quickened, and she moistened her lips with the tip of her tongue. "That would be very nice, thank you."

CHAPTER 7

For the last ten minutes, Judith had been sitting inside Baker's Café with Ernie and his children, and so far the only words Ernie had spoken were to the waitress when she took their order.

If he wasn't going to talk to me, then why did he invite me to join them for supper? Of course, I'm not doing such a good job of making conversation, either.

Judith hated to admit it, but she was attracted to Ernie. There was only one problem—she was sure Ernie didn't feel the same way about her. For that matter, no man had ever shown an interest in her, and she knew why.

She lifted her glass and took a sip of water, hoping the action might help her think about something other than how handsome Ernie was and how homely she must seem to him. *He probably thinks I'm a lonely old maid schoolteacher and only included me in this meal because it was Grace's idea.*

The tantalizing aroma of sizzling steaks caused Judith's stomach to rumble, and she drank more water to tide her over until the food arrived. *Where is that waitress? I'm hungry and so nervous I feel like I might faint.*

Judith glanced over at Grace. The girl's elbows were on the table, and her chin rested in the palm of her hands. Judith fought the urge to mention that it wasn't polite to lean on the table. *She's Ernie's daughter, not mine. He probably wouldn't appreciate me correcting the girl when he's sitting right here.*

The child offered her a wide smile. "It's sure nice havin' ya eat with us, Teacher. Wish we could do this every night."

Judith's cheeks warmed. "It's nice for me, too." She looked at Ernie, wondering if he would say something, but he merely smiled then looked away.

She sighed. *I wish I'd had the good sense to go home after we left the doctor's office.*

Ernie toyed with his fork as he stared across the table at Judith. Grace sat beside her, and Andy was seated next to Ernie. The children had been chatting with one another, but Ernie felt too nervous and tongue-tied to say anything sensible to Judith. He didn't know what had come over him when he'd invited her to join them for supper. Being around the pretty schoolteacher made him feel so scruffy and dim-witted.

He thought about his late wife and how she used to make him feel. Anna had been quiet, meek, and pretty—but in a plain sort of way. She'd been the daughter of a lock tender and hadn't received any more education than Ernie. He'd loved her, though, and would never regret the years they'd had together.

Ernie wondered if his attraction to Judith King went deeper than her physical beauty. *Maybe I'm interested in her because I know I can't have her. Sort of like the fish in the canal that can never live on land.*

He chanced another peek at Judith, and she offered him a brief smile but then looked quickly away. Did she feel as nervous as he did this evening?

Sure wish our food would come. At least then we'd have somethin' to do besides sit here and stare at each other.

Ernie was relieved when Grace leaned over and said something to her teacher. That left Andy free to talk to him. "How's that arm feelin', son?" he asked. "Does it still hurt real bad?"

"Naw, it'll be okay." Andy shook his head, but his pained expression told Ernie he wasn't quite as brave as he pretended to be.

"You gonna be able to do your schoolwork with your left hand?"

Andy frowned. "I don't write so well even with my right hand, so I'll probably make a mess of things when I try to use the other one."

"We could spend time in the evenings practicin'," Ernie suggested.

"Yeah, maybe so." The boy leaned closer to his father and whispered, "I'm wantin' to write somethin' to put in Miss King's letter box."

Ernie smiled. "I'm sure you'll do fine. Just take your time as you print each letter." He reached for his glass of water and took a drink. *If I was one of Judith's pupils, I know what I'd say.*

The following day, Judith waited until school was dismissed to check the letter box. Roger, the boy who had pushed Andy off the porch, had been sent outside to chop wood as his punishment. She'd kept two other boys, Garth and Eric, after school to write essays because they had talked out of turn today. While the boys worked, Judith planned to answer the recent letters she'd received, putting those that were unsigned in the second box inside the coatroom and saving the others to hand out to the students who had signed their names.

Judith pulled the first one out and read it silently.

Dear Teacher:

How come Beth gets to play the part of Mary in the Christmas program?

Ruby

She turned the paper over and wrote on the back:

Dear Ruby:

Beth is older, and there are more lines for her to speak.

I think you will make a sweet little angel.

Miss King

The next letter brought a smile to Judith's lips.

Dear Teacher:

Is it true that a giraffe sleeps standing up? Can I sleep that way, too?

Andy

Judith noticed the boy's disjointed letters. It must have been difficult for him to print with his left hand. She flipped the paper over and wrote the following reply:

Dear Andy:

The book I have about giraffes says they do sleep standing up. Horses and mules do that sometimes, too. If we tried to sleep while still on our feet, we would lose our balance and fall over.

Miss King

There was one more letter in the box, and this one was not signed. It read:

Dear Teacher:

I think you're smart and very purty.

Judith heard some snickering and glanced at the back of

the room. Eric and Garth had their heads together, and she wondered if they knew something about the unsigned letter. Perhaps one of them had written it as a practical joke. It had to be a prank, because she was sure none of her students thought she was pretty.

She rose from her chair and marched over to the boys. "What's so funny, and why are you out of your seats?"

"Nothin's funny. We was just talkin'." Garth wrinkled his nose, Eric looked kind of sheepish, but they both scampered back to their desks.

"Are you finished with your essays?" she questioned.

"Not yet," Eric replied.

"Almost," said Garth.

Judith glanced at the clock on the far wall. "Please get them done, or you'll be late getting home for supper." She moved back to her desk, and the unsigned letter caught her attention again. Should she respond to it, and if so, what should she say?

Pursing her lips, she picked up her pencil.

Dear Student:

It's nice to know that you think I'm smart and pretty. No one has ever told me that before.

Miss King

She held the end of the pencil between her teeth. *Should I have said that? If this letter was written by one of the troublemakers, anything I say could be used in their next joke.*

Quickly, she erased what she had written and started over.

Dear Student:

It's nice to know that you think I'm smart and pretty.

Thank you,

Miss King

Ernie stepped into the small clapboard house he shared with his children during the winter months. It had been a long day, and he was tired and chilled clear to the bone.

"How's your arm?" he asked Andy, who sat on the living room floor in front of the woodstove, reading a book.

"Gettin' better, Papa."

Ernie bent over and ruffled the boy's hair. "Glad to hear it." He glanced around the room. "Where's your sister?"

"When we got home from school, Grace said she was tired, so she went to her room to take a nap."

"Okay." Ernie squatted down beside his son. "How was school today? Did everything go okay?"

Andy shrugged. "Same as always."

"That's good."

"Think we can eat supper with Miss King again?"

Ernie stiffened. He wanted that, too. Fact was, he'd give most anything to spend more time with Judith.

"Papa? Did ya hear what I said?" Andy persisted.

"Yeah, I heard."

"Can we ask her then?"

Ernie blew out his breath. "We'll have to wait and see."

CHAPTER 3

Christmas was only a few days away, and an air of excitement had filled the school for the past week. Judith had dismissed her class nearly an hour ago and had almost finished cleaning the schoolhouse when she heard a *thump, thump* on the porch. Had one of the children forgotten the gift he'd made for his parents?

She rushed to the door, and when she opened it, a gust of chilly air blew in, sending shivers up her spine. To her surprise, no student waited on the porch. It was Ernie Snyder, and he stood beside a perfectly shaped pine tree that was nearly as tall as him. "I was on my way home from work and saw this growin' along one section of the canal. Thought you'd like it for the Christmas program," he mumbled, looking down at his snow-covered boots.

"Oh Ernie, this is so nice. I wasn't sure if we would even have a tree, and it will certainly make the room look more festive."

He only nodded in reply.

"Are Grace and Andy with you?" Judith glanced into the schoolyard, thinking the children might be playing in the snow.

He shook his head. "Naw, they're at home."

She opened the door wider. "Please, bring it inside and come warm yourself by the woodstove."

Ernie brushed the snow off his jacket—the same threadbare one he'd been wearing since the canal closed for the winter. "I ain't so cold." He bounced the tree up and down and gave it a good shake before stepping inside. "Didn't wanna track too much snow into the schoolhouse."

Judith laughed and shut the door behind him. "This floor has gotten snow, mud, and all sorts of other things on it. I don't think a little bit more will hurt."

"Where do ya want the tree?" Ernie questioned.

"How about there?" Judith pointed to the far corner of the room. "We don't want it too close to the stove."

"No, that wouldn't be good." Ernie lifted the tree like it weighed no more than a baby and hauled it across the room. "Have ya got a bucket?"

"A bucket?" Judith placed both hands against her flushed cheeks. She didn't know why she felt so flustered whenever she was around Ernie, but being alone with him made her insides feel all quivery.

"Got to have somethin' to hold the tree upright," Ernie said. "It'll need some water so's it don't dry out."

"I—I suppose we could use the mop bucket I keep in the back room. I think it's big enough to do the job." Judith headed in that direction and returned a few minutes later. She handed Ernie the large metal bucket.

He set the tree inside, but when he let go, it teetered and almost fell over. He grabbed it before it hit the floor. "Guess I'm not thinkin' straight. We're gonna need some rocks in the bucket to hold the tree in place."

"There are plenty of rocks in the schoolyard, but they're buried under the snow," Judith said with a frown.

"That's no problem." Ernie leaned the tree against the wall. Then he grabbed the bucket and headed out the door. Several minutes later, he returned. His face and hands were bright red, and Judith realized he wasn't wearing any gloves.

Ernie dumped the rocks onto the floor, picked up the tree, and positioned it in the middle of the bucket. "Would ya mind holdin' onto the tree, while I put the rocks in place?"

"No. . .no, not at all." Judith held the tree steady as, one by one, he dropped the rocks into the bucket.

"There, that oughta do it. You can let go now."

Judith eased her fingers off the trunk and stepped slowly away. Ernie was right—the tree stayed in place. "It looks good." She moved to one side and appraised their efforts. "Tomorrow the students can decorate it with paper chains and strings of popcorn."

Ernie added water to the bucket, then pointed to the floor where he'd dumped the rocks. "Sorry 'bout the mess. If you'll tell me where ya keep the mop, I'll clean it up."

"Oh, that's all right. I was in the process of cleaning anyhow."

He glanced around the room. "Looks like you're purty well done."

She reached up to push aside a wayward strand of hair that had escaped her bun and nodded. "Yes, I was almost done, but I'll just mop up the mess and be on my way home."

Ernie opened his mouth, like he might argue with her, but then he clamped it shut and moved toward the door. Instead of opening it, however, he dragged the toe of his boot across the floor, making a scraping sound.

"Will you be free to come to the school program tomorrow evening?" she asked.

He nodded. "I'm aimin' to."

"I'm sure your children will be glad. Andy is one of the shepherds, and Grace has the part of an angel."

"So I heard."

Judith was tempted to open the door and order the man out so she could finish cleaning and have a chance to calm down before heading to the Jacobses', but she knew that would be rude. Instead, she stood off to one side with her arms folded, waiting to see what he would do or say next.

Ernie finally grabbed hold of the doorknob. "Guess I'd best be gettin' home. The kids will start to worry if I ain't there soon." After a long pause, he added, "I'll be makin' Andy's favorite meal—fried potatoes and ham. Don't make it nearly as well as my wife used to, but it fills the hole." With that, he stuffed his hands into his jacket pockets and ambled out the door.

"Thanks for the tree," Judith called to his retreating form.

His only response was a backward wave.

She closed the door and leaned against it with a sigh. "That man is so hard to figure out. One thing I do know is he cares about his children."

"You need to calm yourselves down some," Ernie said to his kids as they headed to the schoolhouse the following night for the program. "You two have been jumpin' around like a couple of squirrels ever since we left home."

"I'm scared I'll mess up my part," Andy told his father.

"Well, there's nothin' to be nervous about," Ernie asserted. "You've been practicin' your lines for weeks, and not once have ya messed up."

"Didn't have no audience at home," the boy muttered.

"You'll do fine, just wait and see."

"I ain't nervous," Grace put in. "But I am excited 'bout the candy Miss King is gonna give everyone after the play."

Ernie smiled. Judith certainly liked her pupils, and from what he could tell, they liked her, too.

By the time they got to the schoolhouse, Andy and Grace had calmed down. The room was full of parents—some who'd crammed into their children's desks—others who stood at the back of the room, prepared to watch the play.

"Where's all the kids?" Ernie asked his son.

"Must be in the coatroom. That's where Miss King said we was supposed to put our costumes on over our clothes."

"Guess you'd better get in there." Ernie found a place at the back of the room, and his children disappeared into the coatroom.

A short time later, Judith appeared wearing a long red skirt and a white blouse with lace around the cuffs. Ernie thought she'd never looked more beautiful, and he couldn't help but stare.

Judith welcomed everyone and introduced each child who had a speaking part. Next came the pageant, complete with Nativity scene.

Ernie felt a sense of pride when his kids said their parts without missing a word. They might not be as smart or be dressed as well as some of the other students, but at least they hadn't done or said anything to make them look stupid.

All the parents seemed to enjoy the program, and afterward, during a time of refreshments, Ernie poured a glass of punch and handed it to his son. "Give this to your teacher, would ya?"

Andy's forehead wrinkled. "Why don't ya take it to her yourself, Papa?"

Ernie shook his head. "Naw. It'd be better comin' from you."

Andy shrugged, took the glass, and started across the room.

Ernie stood beside the Christmas tree, now decorated from top to bottom, and watched as the boy handed his teacher the punch. Judith smiled, said something to Andy, and then looked Ernie's way. He felt the heat of a blush creep up his neck and sweep onto his cheeks, so he quickly averted his gaze. Had Andy told his teacher the punch was his dad's idea? *Naw. My boy knows better than to say somethin' like that.*

CHAPTER 9

As the weeks moved on, Judith was pleased that the letter box continued to work well and that the children asked more questions about things pertaining to their education. However, she was troubled by some of the unsigned letters she had received. She suspected that one of her students might have a crush on her. She'd taken it lightly at first, answering each of those letters with some comment about her being glad the student liked her. The letter she'd gotten this morning, however, was a bit harder to answer. It read:

Dear Teacher:

My heart beats like a hammer and my hands get all

sweaty whenever you're near. If it were possible, I'd ask ya to marry me some day.

Judith squinted at the letters on the page. She hadn't been able to match the handwriting to any of her students, but she figured whoever wrote the letter was probably not using the hand he normally wrote with. She'd thought for a while it could be Andy, since his arm had been in a sling for a few days. But Andy was better now and had been using his right hand for several weeks.

She needed to call a halt to this before it went any further, so she picked up her pencil and wrote the following reply:

Dear Student:

I'm flattered that you wish you could marry me. However, I'm too old for you, and I'm your teacher, not your girlfriend. I think it would be best if you only wrote letters with questions about things we are learning in class.

Miss King

The *splat* of a snowball hit the front window, and Judith knew it was time for the students to come in from their morning recess. She left her desk to open the front door, and a blast of frigid air hit her full in the face. How could the children stand to play in such cold weather?

Judith rang the bell, and her pupils filed into the room, talking, laughing, and shaking snow off their coats, hats, and mittens. After putting their wraps inside the coatroom, they took their seats.

Judith scrutinized the desks and realized one child was missing. Where was Grace Snyder? Had she gone to the outhouse or not heard the bell?

She opened the front door and peered into the schoolyard. Several feet from the porch, Grace was sprawled in the snow, moving her arms and legs up and down.

"Recess is over and you need to come inside," Judith called to the child.

Grace hopped up and raced over to another untouched snowy area. "In a minute, Teacher. I'm makin' twin snow angels."

"You can do that at noon or during afternoon recess."

Grace folded her arms and pouted. "I wanna do it now."

The child had never carried on like this before, and Judith was taken by surprise. "I'm only going to say this once more. Come inside."

Grace shook her head. "Not till the snow angels are done."

Unmindful of her long skirt or the fact that she had no wrap on, Judith trudged through the snow and took hold of Grace's arm. "Since you disobeyed, you'll have to stay after school and clean the blackboard."

Grace burst into tears. "I don't wanna do that!"

"Then you should have come inside when I asked you to."

The child sniffled all the way to the schoolhouse and even after she had removed her coat, hat, and mittens.

Judith knew she couldn't allow any of her students to talk

back or defy the rules. Hopefully by tomorrow, Grace would realize that her teacher was also her friend.

"You've gotta go to the schoolhouse with me tomorrow mornin', Papa!" Grace shouted when Ernie arrived home from work and found his children huddled in front of the woodstove.

He bent over and scooped the little girl into his arms. "What's all this about me needin' to go to the schoolhouse?"

"I want ya to talk with Teacher. She's mean, and I don't like her no more."

Ernie lifted his brows. "What's the problem?"

"Aw, she's just mad 'cause Miss King made her stay after school and clean the blackboard," Andy said, stepping up to his father.

Ernie was puzzled. Grace had never been in trouble with the teacher before. In fact, ever since she'd received the sack of candy from Judith after the Christmas program, all Grace could talk about was how sweet her teacher was. "Tell me what happened, daughter."

Tears pooled in the girl's brown eyes. "She said I couldn't make snow angels."

Ernie clenched his teeth. Why would anyone deny a child the right to make an angel in the snow? This didn't sound like something Judith would do, but he needed to find out.

He placed Grace on the floor. "I'll take you and your brother to school tomorrow, and we'll get to the bottom of this."

Judith was surprised when she saw Ernie walk up the snowy path toward the schoolhouse with Grace and Andy at his side. He hadn't accompanied them in quite a while, and she wondered if he'd come today because it was snowing hard again and he felt concern for their safety.

She lifted her hand in a friendly wave. "Good morning, Ernie. Good morning, children."

"'Mornin'," Ernie mumbled as Grace and Andy clomped up the steps and slipped past Judith. "Can I. . .uh. . .have a word with ya?"

"Certainly. Would you like to step inside where it's warmer?"

He shuffled his boots across the frozen snow, and it crunched beneath his weight. "Guess it wouldn't be good to keep ya out here in the cold, but what I got to say probably shouldn't be said in front of the kids."

"Why don't we talk inside the coatroom?" she suggested.

"That's fine."

Judith stepped into the schoolhouse and led the way to the coatroom, near the back of the building. "I need to ask one of the older students to keep an eye on the class," she told Ernie. "If you'd like to wait inside, I'll only be a minute."

Ernie shrugged and offered a quick nod.

Judith leaned over Beth's desk and asked the girl to read a story to the children.

"Sure, Miss King."

"Thank you, Beth." She smiled and hurried to the coatroom, where she found Ernie pacing between the coatrack and the shelves where the letter boxes sat.

"What did you wish to speak with me about?" she asked.

He twisted his stocking cap between his fingers and cleared his throat. "Grace told me ya kept her after school yesterday. Said it was 'cause she wanted to make snow angels."

"That's true."

"You got somethin' against snow angels, Miss King?"

Judith frowned. Miss King? Why had Ernie reverted to calling her Miss King?

"I have nothing against snow angels, Mr. Snyder," she said, emphasizing his last name. "However, your daughter wanted to make them after recess was over."

He stared at the floor. "She was wrong to disobey, but she's only a little girl. Don't ya think ya could have been a bit easier on her? I mean, forcin' her to stay after school to clean the blackboard made her think ya don't like her."

Judith folded her arms and released a sigh. "I care about all my students, but I can't make exceptions for anyone who disobeys the rules."

Ernie looked up again, and the intensity of his gaze sent chills down her back. "It's been hard for my kids to grow up without a mother. Can't ya see that?"

She nodded, as tears filled her eyes and memories from the past flooded her mind. "I understand better than you know, for my own mother died when I was ten years old."

His forehead wrinkled, and he reached up to rub the bridge of his nose. "Sorry. I didn't know."

Judith took a few steps forward, bringing herself close enough to the man that she could feel the warmth of his breath. She shivered.

"Ya cold?"

"No, no. I'm fine." She rubbed her hands briskly over her arms. "Ernie, I'm sure you love your children."

"Ya got that right."

"But you can't baby them. They need to know there are consequences when they do something wrong."

"I discipline my kids when they do somethin' bad." He lifted his chin. "But I don't think playin' in the snow a few minutes longer'n you would've liked was such a terrible thing. You was wrong, Miss King!"

Judith's defenses rose higher. Was this man questioning her ability to teach the students right from wrong? He had said he was a Christian and had taught his children memory verses. He'd been going to church fairly regularly, too. So why was he talking to her this way? Maybe Ernie Snyder wasn't the man she'd thought him to be.

She blew out her breath. "I was hired to teach here, so until the school board says otherwise, it's up to me to decide when and how to discipline."

"We'll see 'bout that!" He slapped his hat on his head and stormed out of the coatroom. Judith heard the front door slam shut and knew he had gone.

What have I done? She placed both hands against her hot

cheeks. *Ernie will probably never speak to me again, and he might even decide to pull his children from school before spring. I'd better spend some time praying about this matter.*

CHAPTER 10

Judith had looked for Ernie at church the following Sunday, hoping to apologize for their disagreement. However, he wasn't there, and neither were his children. Grace and Andy showed up for school on Monday morning, and for that, she felt relief.

All weekend she'd been reading her Bible and praying about the situation. She had asked the Lord's forgiveness for snapping at Ernie, but now it was time to offer an apology to Grace's father.

While her students read to themselves, Judith decided to write Ernie a note. She opened her desk drawer, took out a piece of paper and a pencil, then wrote the following message:

Dear Ernie:

I've been thinking about the discussion we had last week concerning Grace and her refusal to come inside after recess. I'm sorry for our difference of opinion. I shouldn't have spoken to you in such a disagreeable tone.

I care about all of my students. When I kept Grace after school, I was only doing what I felt was best. But as her parent, you had the right to ask me about it.

Your children speak highly of you, and I'm glad you're teaching them God's ways, for His Word is our best teacher.

I realize it must be difficult for you to raise your children without a wife. From personal experience, I know it's hard for them to be without their mother. Grace and Andy are fortunate to have such a caring, loving father.

I hope you will accept my apology, and I look forward to hearing from you soon.

Sincerely,
Judith King

Judith folded the paper and set it aside. When school was dismissed, she would give the note to Andy and ask him to deliver it to his father. By tomorrow morning, she hoped to receive a reply from Ernie.

Long after his children went to bed, Ernie paced the living room floor, thinking, praying, and worrying. He'd read and reread

Judith's letter so many times he knew some of the phrases by heart—or at least the easier words he could understand.

He stopped in front of the stove and added two more chunks of wood—not because he was cold, but because he hoped the action would take his mind off Judith King. It wasn't bad enough he was an ignorant canaler who was at a loss for words whenever he was with the woman, but now he'd lost his temper in front of her. He should go to the school and apologize in person, but how could he face her after the things he'd said?

"I sure can't write the teacher no letter," Ernie mumbled as he shut the door on the stove. "She'd really think I'm a dunce if I did somethin' like that."

He moved to the window and stared out at the night sky. Several inches of snow remained on the ground—he could see it glistening in the moonlight. Soon spring would be here, and then he could return to the canal. Things would be better once his kids were out of school. He'd have less chance of running into Judith and getting all tongue-tied and squirrelly.

Ernie hadn't known Judith very long, but during the time they had spent together, he'd seen her patience and kindness toward his children. Andy and Grace often came home from school with stories of the interesting things their teacher had said or done. It was evident that Judith cared about her students and enjoyed being a teacher. He knew that included disciplining when it became necessary.

Whenever Ernie had taken his children to church, he'd watched Judith from a distance. She listened intently to the preacher and always had her Bible open during the reading of the scriptures. There was a look of peace on her face as she sat in the pew singing praises to God. It was a look he could get used to seeing on a daily basis.

Ernie groaned. "I need to apologize to her."

"You got a letter for me to give the teacher?" Andy asked his father the following morning.

Ernie shook his head. "Nope."

"But she wrote you yesterday, and I thought—"

"This ain't none of your business." Ernie gave Andy a pat on the head. "I'll handle things with Miss King in my own way."

"I could sneak the note into the letter box, so the other kids wouldn't know, and then—"

"No."

"Okay." Andy grabbed his lunch pail and turned to face his sister. "Ready, Grace?"

"I'm comin'." Grace gave Ernie a hug and scampered out the door.

"Have a good day at school!" Ernie called to his children.

A few minutes later, he donned his coat, hat, and gloves, then headed out the door. He still hadn't decided how to go about apologizing to Judith, but he'd worry about that later. Right now there was some ice waiting to be cut.

Judith stood at the front door as her students filed into the room. She smiled at Andy and waited expectantly to see if he would hand her a letter. When the boy headed for the coatroom without a word, she began to worry. Maybe Andy hadn't delivered her note to his father. Then again, maybe he had, but Ernie hadn't sent a reply.

Judith didn't wish to embarrass the boy in front of the others, so she waited until morning recess to broach the subject. Andy made it easy for her when he was the last one out the door.

"May I speak to you a moment?" she asked him.

He turned around. "What about? Have I done somethin' wrong?"

She shook her head and motioned him back inside. "I want to ask you a question."

Andy leaned against the nearest desk and stared up at her.

"I was wondering if you delivered my letter to your father yesterday?"

He nodded.

"Did he write me a note in return?"

Andy shook his head.

"Did he ask you to tell me anything this morning?"

"Nope. Just said to have a good day at school."

Judith sighed. If Ernie hadn't sent a note or given Andy a verbal message, he must still be angry with her. Was he planning to speak with the school board about the rules she'd made? Would he try to get her fired?

"Is that all, Teacher?" Andy asked. "I'd like to get outside and help with the snow fort some of the kids are makin'."

"Yes, that's all I had to say. Run along, and tell the others I said to be careful. The snow started to melt yesterday, but now that it's turned cold again, it will probably be slippery."

"I'm used to walkin' in slippery places. Once the ice thaws and the canals open again, there'll be mud and lots of puddles along the towpath."

Judith shuddered. Just thinking about the poor boy trudging up and down the towpath six days a week made her feel sad. He was too young to be put to work like that. And then there was Grace left to run around Ernie's boat with only the supervision of an elderly man.

"Do be careful, Andy," she said as he stepped onto the porch.

"I will."

She shut the door and moved over to the potbellied stove. The room had cooled some, and it was time to add more wood to the fire.

On Friday morning, Ernie made a decision. "I'll be walkin' with you to school today," he announced to his children after breakfast.

Andy looked surprised. "How come, Papa?"

"Need to speak with your teacher."

Grace stared at him with questioning eyes. "Am I in trouble again?"

He reached across the table and took her hand. " 'Course not. I need to say a few things to Miss King."

"Okay." Grace picked up her spoon and delved into the bowl of cornmeal mush set before her.

A short time later, Ernie found himself on the steps of the schoolhouse one more time, asking the teacher if he could have a word with her. At first, Judith looked undecided, but then she gave him a nod. "Come inside."

"In the coatroom again?" he asked, looking in that direction.

"That's probably a good idea."

Ernie waited until Judith instructed the class on what they should do in her absence. Then he followed her to the back room. Once inside, he had second thoughts about his mission. Being in such cramped quarters with her standing so close, he could smell the sweet scent of the soap she'd probably used this morning. His knees began to knock.

"What did you wish to speak with me about?" she asked.

He shuffled his feet a couple of times, then decided to plunge ahead. "I got your note."

Her only reply was a brief nod.

"I. . .uh. . .want ya to know that there's no hard feelin's."

She smiled. "I'm glad."

"And. . .I–I'm sorry for spoutin' off the last time we talked. I had no call to get so upset."

Judith opened her mouth as if to say something, but Ernie hurried on before he lost his nerve. "You were right about Grace. She shouldn't have disobeyed the rules. She deserved to be punished, too." There, that felt better.

She extended her hand. "I'm glad you understand."

When his fingers curled around hers, it felt like a bolt of

lightning had shot up his arm. He pulled away quickly, and Judith did the same. Then she lowered her hand and smoothed her long gingham dress as though there might be wrinkles. "Thank you for coming, Ernie. I know you have a job to do, so I mustn't keep you any longer."

"No, it's me who shouldn't be takin' your time. You've got a class waitin'." He moved toward the door but turned back around. "You're a good teacher, and I'm glad my kids have been in your class this winter. I'm sure they'll miss ya come spring."

"I wish they didn't have to drop out of school when the canal opens again," she said. "They'll miss so much and will probably have to repeat the same grade when they return next winter."

He shrugged. "I only made it through the fourth grade, and I'm managin' okay. Besides, Andy will be walkin' the mules for a few more years, and after that he'll work on the boat with me. Sooner or later, the boat will be his to captain. He don't need much schoolin' for that."

Judith's wrinkled forehead told him she didn't agree, but she never offered a word of argument.

"Have a nice day," Ernie said, turning toward the coatroom door.

"You, too."

Ernie grasped the knob and gave it a yank, but the door didn't open. He tried again. Nothing happened. "It seems to be locked," he mumbled.

Judith rushed forward and pulled on the doorknob, but

it didn't budge for her, either. She pounded on the door. "Somebody, please open this!"

Not a sound could be heard, and the door remained firmly shut.

"I'll bet one of those troublemakers who sits near the back of the room decided to lock us in," she said.

Ernie bent down and squinted, as he peered through the keyhole. "Can't see a thing. The key must be in there."

Judith clucked her tongue. "Whoever did this will be cleaning the blackboard until school lets out for the summer." She folded her arms and released a puff of air that lifted her curly bangs right off her forehead.

Ernie fought the temptation to touch one of those curls, wondering if Judith's shiny blond hair was as soft as it appeared. Her pinched expression and squinted eyes made him want to laugh. She looked awful cute when she was mad.

"I wish I knew what I'd done to make one of my students angry enough to lock us in," Judith said.

Ernie rubbed his forehead. He couldn't imagine anyone wanting to get even with her. Judith was a good teacher, and he'd come to realize that her firmness with Grace had been necessary. The child had gotten over her anger, so he was sure she wasn't responsible for this.

The key rattled in the hole, and Ernie and Judith bent toward it at the same time. Their heads collided.

"Ouch!" they said in unison.

"You okay?" he asked, reaching up to feel her forehead. The minute his fingers came in contact with Judith's skin, he wished he hadn't touched her. An unfamiliar jolt shot through him, and his face grew hot and sweaty.

Her eyes were wide as she slowly nodded. "I–I'm fine. How about you?"

"I've got a hard head. I'm sure there ain't no damage."

Suddenly, the door swung open, and Grace rushed into the room. "It was Andy who done it!"

Ernie stepped out of the coatroom and sought out his son.

Andy sat at his desk with his head down. "Sorry, Papa," he mumbled. "I just wanted to make sure you and Miss King stayed in there long enough to patch things up."

Ernie could hardly believe his own son had been the one to lock the door. "Everything's fine between me and the teacher," he muttered, "so the only thing you did is to get yourself in trouble. And now you're gonna have chalk dust on your clothes for a long time to come."

CHAPTER 11

As she stood on the schoolhouse porch, saying good-bye to her canal students on a Friday afternoon in late March, Judith felt as if her heart would break. She was going to miss them all, especially Grace and Andy, for whom she had formed an attachment that went beyond teacher and pupil.

Judith thought about Ernie and how she would miss seeing him at church and various community functions. Now that he was hauling coal up the canal again, it wasn't likely she would see him much at all. He was a good father, and she knew his children belonged with him. But the thought of Andy returning to the hard work of mule driving, Grace running around the boat with little supervision, and the two of them going without schooling for so many months made her sad.

If only there was a way they could receive their education during the spring and fall. Judith turned toward the door, knowing it was time to clean the blackboard and secure the schoolhouse for the weekend. She knew the logical thing was to commit Ernie and his children to the Lord.

As Ernie guided his boat past Parryville, his thoughts went to Judith King. What was she doing right now, and did she ever think of him?

"Why would she?" he muttered. "Even if she knew how I felt, she'd never take an interest in someonc like me."

"You talkin' to yourself, boss?" Jeb called from the center of the boat, where he stood in front of the small cookstove.

"Yeah, guess I was."

Jeb grunted and kept stirring the pot of stew he'd started some time ago.

Ernie glanced at the shoreline, and his breath caught in his throat. Judith sat under a tree not far from the towpath. Her long blond hair lay across her shoulders like a ray of golden sunlight. Andy approached her and halted the mules. Any other time Ernie would have hollered at the boy to keep moving, but he was as anxious to see his kids' schoolteacher as they were.

Judith joined Andy in the middle of the towpath, and a short time later, Ernie had the boat docked near the shore. He'd no more than set the gangplank in place, when Grace bounded off the boat and rushed over to Judith. "Teacher! Teacher! It's mighty nice to see ya!"

Judith bent over and gave Grace a hug. "I'm happy to see you and Andy, too." She smiled at Ernie, who now stood beside his children. "Hello, Ernie."

He swallowed around his Adam's apple and nodded. "How have ya been?"

She pushed a windblown strand of hair away from her face. "I'm fine. How are you and the children?"

He wiped his forehead with the back of his shirtsleeve, wondering if he looked as dirty and sweaty as he felt. "Fine. We're all fine. Keepin' busy, as usual."

"Papa's hopin' to make enough money so's me and Grace can have new boots for school come winter," Andy interjected.

Judith smiled. "That's good. It's always nice to have something new."

"What are ya doin' down here by the canal?" Grace asked, voicing the question that had been on the tip of Ernie's tongue.

"I thought it would be nice to enjoy a Saturday afternoon near the water. I brought along a picnic lunch and have been watching the boats go by." She motioned to the wicker basket on the blanket where she had been sitting.

"Wish we could have a picnic," Grace said with a pout. "I get tired of stayin' on the boat all the time."

"Yeah," Andy agreed. "It'd be awful nice to eat somethin' besides Jeb's funny-tastin' soups and gritty stews."

"What do you do on the boat?" Judith asked, touching Grace's shoulder.

Grace wrinkled her nose. "Ain't much to do 'cept play with the corn-husk dolly Papa gave me. Sometimes I just watch the other boats go past."

"Isn't, not ain't," Judith corrected.

Ernie shifted from one leg to the other. *I say ain't all the time. She probably thinks I'm really a dunce.*

"You still usin' the letter box, Teacher?" Andy asked, changing the subject.

She nodded. "We are, but there aren't as many unsigned letters as there used to be."

Ernie wiped his sweaty palms on the sides of his trousers. "Well, guess we'd best be goin'. Won't get that load of coal hauled up to Easton if we keep on jawin'."

Judith's eyes were downcast, and there was a tiny crease between her brows. She was no doubt missing Andy and Grace and probably wished they could be in school all year.

"Aw, Papa, do we hafta go so soon?" Grace whined. "I'd like to visit with Teacher awhile."

"Same here," Andy agreed.

Judith placed both hands on top of the children's heads. "You'd best do as your father says. Maybe I'll see you sometime this summer." She turned to face Ernie. "Might you be coming to church in Parryville soon?"

He shrugged. "Don't rightly know. Guess it all depends on where we stop on a Saturday night."

"I understand."

Grace gave her teacher another hug, then trudged back to the boat.

"Be careful to stay away from the edge," Judith called to the child.

"I will."

"Between Jeb and me, we keep an eye on the girl."

"Yes, I'm sure you do, but—"

Ernie gave his son a pat on the back. "Get them mules movin', son. They've had a long enough rest." He lifted his hand. "See ya, Judith."

When school was out for the summer, Judith often went for walks along the towpath, where she watched the boats and hoped to see Ernie and his children go by. Sometimes, on hot, muggy days like this one, she would take off her shoes and wade in the cool water. It was also a good time to read her Bible, pray, and contemplate the future.

Judith stopped walking long enough to watch a pair of ducks settle on the water.

" 'Male and female created he them,' " she quoted from Genesis. "Will I ever find a mate, or will I spend the rest of my days as an old maid?"

Judith moved on, wondering if God might have something else in mind for her besides teaching at the schoolhouse. *I'm in love with Ernie and care deeply for his children, but he's given me no indication that he feels the same way toward me.* She sniffed and forced her tears to remain in check. *Dear Lord, help me learn to be content.*

"Simmer down and quit your runnin'!" Ernie hollered at his

daughter as she scampered from the bow of the boat to the stern and back again. He glanced around, hoping Jeb would find something for her to do, but the elderly man was nowhere in sight. "Must have gone below to get somethin'," he muttered. "He'd better not be sleepin' on the job again."

Ernie guided the boat through the locks, glad when it went well and the mules cooperated. It would have been easier if Jeb had been on deck to keep an eye out for other boats and be sure they weren't getting too close.

They'd only gone a short way past the locks when Ernie heard a splash. Thinking it must be some kid throwing a rock into the canal, he continued to steer the boat as it moved forward.

"Help! Papa, help me!"

Ernie froze.

"Get her, Papa! Grace is drownin'!" Andy shouted from the towpath.

Ernie rushed to the side of the boat and looked over. He saw nothing but the swirling waters and a tree branch bobbing up and down.

"She's over there!" Andy hollered, pointing to the water splashing against the bow of the boat.

Ernie made a beeline in that direction and dove into the chilly canal. He spotted Grace a few feet away, her arms pawing the water, her legs kicking frantically. Down she went, then up again, gurgling, screaming, panting for air.

He reached her seconds before she went under again and wrapped his arm around her chest. Several minutes later they were on the shore, Grace gasping for breath, Ernie thanking God he'd gotten to his daughter in time.

Once they were on the boat again, Ernie made sure Grace changed into dry clothes and went to bed. Then he headed for Jeb's sleeping quarters and found the man sprawled on his bunk, fast asleep.

Ernie grimaced and shook Jeb's shoulders. "Wake up!"

His helper's eyes popped open, and he released a noisy yawn. "What's the matter, boss? How come you're all wet?"

Ernie quickly explained about Grace falling overboard, and Jeb's face blanched. "It's my fault. If I'd been up there watchin' her instead of takin' a nap, she never would have fallen off the boat."

Ernie couldn't argue with that, but yelling at his helper wouldn't change what had happened.

Jeb sat up and swung his legs over the edge of the bunk. "It's time for me to put myself out to pasture."

Ernie's eyebrows lifted. "What are you talkin' about?"

"I should have stayed in Easton with my daughter and not returned to the canal this spring. I'm gettin' too old to be watchin' out for a little one while I try to cook, clean, and keep an eye out for boats that might be comin' ahead." Jeb shook his head. "Ya need someone younger'n smarter'n me. What ya really need is a wife."

Ernie stood there a few seconds, letting Jeb's comments run through his befuddled brain. Finally, with a feeling of determination, he tapped the elderly man on the shoulder and said, "I think ya might be right 'bout some of that. And

I believe it's time for me to take action."

"Teacher, there's somebody here to see you!"

Judith looked up from where she sat on the sofa, darning a pair of long black stockings. "Who is it, Melody?" she asked the preacher's daughter.

"It's that canal boatman."

"Who?"

"Andy and Grace's pa."

Judith's heart thudded in her chest, as she stood on trembling legs. Had Ernie come to pay her a call? *Of course not, don't be ridiculous.* She went to the door and found him standing on the porch with his arms crossed. "Hello, Ernie. I'm surprised to see you."

He rocked back and forth on the heels of his boots. "I. . . um. . .that is. . ."

"What is it?" she prompted.

"The other day Grace fell overboard and almost drowned."

Judith gasped and covered her mouth with the back of her hand. "Is she all right?"

Ernie nodded. "My helper fell asleep and wasn't watchin' her. Now he's plannin' to move to Easton to live with his daughter, and that leaves me with no one to mind Grace." He stared at the porch. "You were right about her needin' more supervision."

Judith didn't know how best to reply, so she just stood there.

"The thing is. . .I. . .uh. . .well, I think we should get married!"

"What?" Judith felt the blood drain from her face. Had she heard him right? Had Ernie just asked her to marry him?

"I said, I think. . .I mean, would ya marry me?" he stammered.

Judith grasped the doorknob, feeling as though she could topple over. She had wished so long that someone might propose to her, but she never thought it would happen—and certainly not like this! What about love? What about romance? Could she marry Ernie simply because he needed a mother for his children? He obviously didn't love her, or he would have said so. And what about her teaching job? If she were to marry, she would have to give that up. No, it was impossible, and she told him so.

He blanched. "I thought you cared about my kids."

"I do."

"Then what's the problem?"

Judith fought the desire to tell Ernie how much she loved him, but that would be the worst thing she could do. "I hope you're able to find a suitable replacement for Jeb—someone who will be able to watch out for Grace." She gathered the edge of her skirt, turned, and rushed inside.

CHAPTER 12

After a sleepless night, Judith wasn't sure she could go to church the following morning. As she stood in front of her bedroom mirror, she realized that her eyes were rimmed with red, her cheeks looked puffy, and her nose was sore from having blown it so much. When Ernie left yesterday, she'd gone to her room and cried until no more tears would come.

How could the man expect her to marry him when there was no love involved? She knew he needed someone to cook, clean, and watch out for Grace, but surely he could hire a young, able-bodied helper to do those things.

"Then why did he ask me to marry him?" she moaned.

Judith's gaze fell on her Bible lying on the dressing table. It was never good to begin the day without reading God's Word.

She picked up the Bible, took a seat on her bed, and opened it to Proverbs. One particular verse seemed to jump right out at her. " 'Trust in the Lord with all thine heart; and lean not unto thine own understanding. In all thy ways acknowledge him, and he shall direct thy paths.' "

Judith drew in a deep breath. "I know I should trust You in all things, Lord," she prayed, "but sometimes it's hard to do. Could it be that You might have something else in mind for me other than teaching? Would it be better for Grace and Andy if I were to marry Ernie? Could it be Your will for me to be his wife?"

She moved back to the mirror. "I know I'm not beautiful, but perhaps in time Ernie could come to care for me the way I do him."

Judith remembered hearing Pastor Jacobs's wife tell her daughters that real beauty comes from the inside, not the outward appearance. Perhaps if she allowed God to work through her and set a good example to Ernie's children, he might learn to appreciate her inner beauty.

Judith sat on the grassy bank of the canal, waiting, watching, hoping Ernie's boat would come around the bend. She had been coming here every day for the last week and hadn't spotted him. In the past he'd come by Parryville about the same time of day. Maybe he had been delayed. She knew there were often pileups at the locks, and sometimes breaks in the canal occurred.

"Or maybe he changed his schedule, and I've missed him." She lifted her face to the sun, leaned back on her elbows, and closed her eyes. "Heavenly Father, I'm trusting You to direct my paths. If it's Your will for me to speak with Ernie, then he will come by at the right time."

A sense of peace settled over Judith, and she knew what she must do. When summer was over and the children of Parryville returned to the one-room schoolhouse, would Judith still be their teacher? Her fate was in God's hands.

For the last week, Ernie had been held up a few miles outside of Mauch Chunk, waiting for a break in the canal to be repaired. Normally he would have been upset about the time lost, but the days of waiting had given him time to think and pray—something he should have done before asking Judith to marry him.

When the boats were finally given the go-ahead and they rounded the bend near Parryville, Ernie's heart skipped a beat. Judith sat on the grassy bank, her face lifted to the sky. She looked like an angel.

Ernie maneuvered the boat toward land. "Halt the mules!" he shouted to Andy.

Judith must have heard him, for she stood and rushed toward the boat.

"Stay put. I'll be right back," Ernie said to Grace, who stood next to the rails, hollering and waving at her teacher.

Ernie leaped over the side and waded to shore, not caring

that his trousers and boots were getting wet. Before Judith could open her mouth, he reached into his shirt pocket and pulled out the note he had written. He handed it to her and took a step back.

"What's this?" she asked, tipping her head, a curious expression on her face.

"I have trouble speakin' what's on my heart, so I thought I could say things better this way."

With trembling fingers, Judith unfolded the piece of paper and read Ernie's note.

Dear Judith:

I'm sorry for the dumb things I said the day I asked ya to marry me. I got all tongue-tied and couldn't say everything on my mind. I want us to get married but not just 'cause my kids need a mom. You're the sweetest, purtiest woman I know, and I love ya.

I ain't much to look at, and I don't have much education, but I'd sure be pleased if you was to become my wife.

Love,
Ernie

Judith stared at the letter, tears clouding her vision. Ernie loved her and thought she was pretty. It was more than she could fathom. She blinked the tears away and squinted. *I recognize this handwriting. I've seen it before.* Then a light dawned, and realization set in. "Ernie, have you written to me on other occasions?"

He nodded.

"Did you put some notes in the letter box at school?"

He shook his head.

"No?" Maybe she was wrong. Maybe the handwriting wasn't the same as the anonymous letters she'd received last winter from a secret admirer.

"Papa wrote the letters, but it was me who put 'em in the letter box," Andy spoke up.

Judith stared at the boy, too stunned to say a word.

Ernie stepped forward and took her hand. "I'm sorry for deceivin' ya, but I didn't have the nerve to say those things to your face. Thought ya might think I was dumber'n dirt and that I was bein' too forward."

Judith smiled. "Oh Ernie, do you know how I have longed to hear such words?" She waved the letter in front of his face. "You're not dumb, and I would be honored to be your wife."

He looked surprised. "Really?"

She nodded. "I've come to love you as well."

"Yippee!" Grace hollered as she scampered over the side of the boat and plodded through the water.

When the child reached Judith's side, Judith gave her a hug. "I love you and your brother, too."

Andy grinned from ear to ear, but then his expression sobered. "If ya marry Papa, will ya still be our teacher?"

Judith slowly shook her head. If she married Ernie, it would mean giving up her teaching position, but she felt this was what God wanted her to do.

Ernie snapped his fingers. "Say, I've got an idea."

"What is it?" she asked.

"As we're goin' up and down the canal, whenever we stop for the night, maybe you could give Grace and Andy some lessons—and any other kids whose folks work the canals. That way they won't get behind in their schoolin'."

"I think that's a wonderful idea," she said with a smile.

Ernie cleared his throat. "Uh, Andy, why don't ya unhitch the mules and tie 'em to a tree? Then ya can take Grace back to the boat, so's your teacher and me can make some plans."

Andy grinned up at his father. "Okay."

Once the children were on the boat, Ernie led Judith to a clump of trees a short distance away. There, under a canopy of leafy maple branches, he drew her into his arms and kissed her so tenderly that she thought she might swoon.

Judith closed her eyes and leaned against Ernie's muscular chest. "I thank the Lord for bringing you and your children into my life. Through His Word, God showed me that I need to trust Him in all things."

"I love ya, dear Teacher," Ernie murmured.

"And I love you."

TWICE LOVED

DEDICATION

In memory of my uncle, Dean Thompson, who survived the bombing at Pearl Harbor. To Dr. Bob and Delva Lantrip, who make all their patients feel "Twice Loved." And to my sister, Joy Stenson, who, like Amy in this story, loved to play with dolls and stuffed animals when she was a little girl.

INTRODUCTION

Japan's unconditional surrender to the Allies on September 2, 1945, ended World War II. America and her allies rejoiced. The idea of peace had never seemed more precious than to those who had given faithful service on the home front, as well as those who had served on the battlefield.

Yet much needed to be done before peace could be achieved. Those who had lost loved ones grieved. Families of those who were classified as prisoners of war or missing in action hoped and prayed for the day when their loved ones might return home. Factories that had been engaged in the production of war materials returned to their former pursuits. Thousands of "Rosie the Riveters," women who had replaced men who had been called to defend their country, were no longer needed.

Returning military personnel further flooded the job market.

There was rejoicing and mourning, newly created problems, and the adjustment from war to peace, but the spark of hope that had kept people through the dark days of war, rationing, and personal sacrifice burned high. A weary world looked forward to a season of peace on earth, good will to men.

PROLOGUE

Easton, Pennsylvania
September 1943

Dan Fisher went down on his knees in front of the sofa where his wife lay. Darcy had been diagnosed with leukemia several months earlier, and short of a miracle, he knew she wouldn't have long to live.

"I'm almost finished with this quilt," Darcy murmured, lifting one corner of the colorful patchwork covering she had been working on since she'd first gotten sick. It was made from various shapes of cotton and velveteen material, in shades of blue, scarlet, gold, and green, and had been hand tied. She'd been able to do much of the stitching while lying in bed or on the sofa, where she spent most of her waking hours.

Dan nodded. "It's beautiful, honey—just like you."

"I want you to have it as a remembrance of me." Tears gathered in the corners of Darcy's dark-brown eyes, and she blinked them away. "It will bring you solace after I'm gone and help you remember to comfort others in need."

Unable to voice his thoughts, Dan reached for Darcy's hand. When she squeezed his fingers, he was amazed at the strength of her touch.

"There are things we must discuss," she whispered.

Dan nodded, wishing they could talk about anything other than his wife's imminent death.

"Please promise you'll keep Twice Loved open."

Dan knew how important Darcy's used-toy store was to her and to all the children she had ministered to by providing inexpensive or free toys. Little ones whose fathers were away at war and those who'd been left with only one parent had received a measure of happiness, thanks to Darcy and her special store.

"I'll keep the place going," he promised. "Whenever I look at this quilt, I'll remember the labor of love that went into making it, and I'll do my best to help others in need."

CHAPTER 1

September 1945

Bev Winters shut her desk drawer with such force that the cherished picture of her late husband toppled to the floor. Her hands shook as she bent to retrieve it, but she breathed a sigh of relief to see that the glass was intact and Fred's handsome face smiled back at her.

Joy Lundy poked her head around the partition that separated her and Bev's workspaces in the accounting department at Bethlehem Steel. "What happened, Bev? I heard a crash."

Bev clutched the picture to her chest and sank into the office chair. She reached for the crumpled slip of paper on her desk and handed it to her coworker. "What a nice thing to give someone at the end of the day. I've got two weeks to tie up loose ends and clear out my desk."

Joy scanned the memo, her forehead creasing as she frowned. "I heard there would be some cutbacks, now that the war is over and many of our returning men will need their old jobs back. I just didn't realize it would be so soon—or that you'd be one of those they let go."

Bev pulled the bottom drawer open and scooped up her pocketbook. "It's probably for the best," she mumbled. "I was thinking I might have to look for another job anyway."

"You were? How come?"

Bev hung her head, feeling the humiliation of what had transpired yesterday afternoon.

Joy touched Bev's trembling shoulder. "Tell me what's wrong."

"I—I—It's nothing, really." Bev was afraid to admit that their boss had tried to take advantage of her. What if Joy told someone and the news spread around the building? Bev's reputation could be tarnished, and so would her Christian testimony. Here at Bethlehem Steel she'd tried to tell others about Christ through her actions and by inviting them to attend church. No, it would be best if she kept quiet about what had happened with Frank Martin. She'd be leaving in two weeks anyway.

Joy tapped Bev gently on the shoulder, driving her disconcerting thoughts to the back of her mind. "I'm here if you want to talk."

Bev nodded, as tears clouded her vision. "I–I'd better get going. I don't want to be late picking Amy up at the sitter's."

Joy returned to her own desk, and Bev left the office. Bev

had only taken a few steps when she bumped into a tall man with sandy-blond hair. She didn't recognize him and figured he must not work here or could be a returning veteran—perhaps the one who would be taking her bookkeeping position.

When the man looked down, Bev noticed that the latch on his briefcase had popped open, and several black-and-white photographs were strewed on the floor.

"I'm so sorry," she apologized.

"It's my fault. I wasn't watching where I was going." He squatted down and began to collect the pictures. "I'm here to do a photo shoot for management and can't find the conference room. Do you know where it is?"

"Two doors down. Here, let me help you with those." Bev knelt on the floor, unmindful of her hose that already had a small tear in them. As she helped gather the remaining photos, she almost collided with the man's head.

For a few seconds, he stared at Bev with a look of sympathy. Could he tell she'd been crying? Did he think she was clumsy for bumping into him, causing his briefcase to open?

She handed the man his photos and stood, smoothing her dark-green, knee-length skirt. "Sorry about the pictures. I hope none of them are ruined."

He put the photos back into his briefcase, snapped it closed, and rose. "No harm done. Thanks for your help."

"You're welcome."

The man hesitated a moment, like he wanted to say something more, but then he strode down the hallway toward the conference room.

Bev headed in the opposite direction, anxious to get her daughter and head for home.

As Dan strolled down the hallway, he thought about the young woman he'd bumped into a few minutes ago. She wore her dark hair in a neat pageboy and had the bluest eyes he'd ever seen. If he wasn't mistaken, there'd been tears in her eyes, and he figured she must have been crying before they collided.

It's none of my business, he admonished himself. *My desire to help others sometimes clouds my judgment.*

Dan spotted the conference room and was about to open the door, when a middle-aged man with a balding head stopped him. "Hey, aren't you Dan Fisher?"

Puzzled, Dan only nodded in reply.

"I'm Pete Mackey. We met back in '39 when we were photographing the pedestrian suspension bridge that links Warren and Valley Streets. That was shortly after it was damaged by a severe storm."

"I remember. That was quite a mess," Dan said. "The new bridge is holding together nicely though."

"Yeah, until the next hurricane hits the coast."

"I hope not."

Pete's pale eyebrows drew together. "Say, didn't you lose your wife a few years ago? I remember reading her obituary in the newspaper."

"Darcy died of leukemia in the fall of '43." Dan's skin prickled. He hated to think about how he'd lost his precious wife, much less discuss his feelings with a near stranger.

"That must have been rough."

"It was."

"Do you have any children?"

"No, but we wanted some."

"Me and the wife have five." Pete gave his left earlobe a couple of pulls. "Kids can be a handful at times, but I wouldn't trade mine for anything."

Dan smiled and glanced at his watch. In about two minutes he would be late for his appointment.

"You here on business?" Pete asked.

"Yes. I've been asked to photograph some of the managers. How about you?"

"Came to interview a couple of women who lost their husbands in the war."

"I see. Well it was nice seeing you again." Dan turned toward the door, hoping Pete would take the hint and be on his way.

"Say, I was wondering if you could do me a favor," Pete said.

Dan glanced over his shoulder. "What's that?"

"I'm working for *Family Life Magazine* now, and I've been asked to write an article on how people deal with grief. Since you lost your wife, I figured you might be able to give me some helpful insights."

Dan pivoted on his heel. "Are you suggesting an interview?"

"Yep. I'm sure the article will reach people all over the country who lost a loved one during the war. Some might be helped by your comments or advice, same as with the folks I'll be interviewing here today."

Dan's face warmed, and his palms grew sweaty. Even though it had been two years since Darcy's death, it was still difficult to talk about. Hardly a day had gone by that he hadn't yearned for her touch. He wasn't ready to share his feelings—not even to help someone going through grief.

"Sorry," Dan mumbled. "I'm not interested in being interviewed for your magazine, and I'm late for an appointment." He hurried off before Pete could say anything more.

CHAPTER 2

Dan leaned against his polished oak office chair and raked his fingers through the back of his hair, preparing to look over some proofs from a recent wedding that he'd done. Things had been busy lately and soon would get even busier, with Christmas only three months away. Many people wanted portraits taken to give as gifts, and he hoped those who did wouldn't wait until the last minute to schedule an appointment. That had happened in the past, and there were days when he wondered why he'd ever become a photographer.

Dan thought about his first career choice and how he had wanted to join the navy shortly after he got out of high school. However, due to a knee injury he'd received playing football, he had been turned down for active duty.

Guess it's just as well, he thought. *If I'd gone into the navy, I might never have met Darcy. Might not be alive today either.*

He thought about the radio broadcasts he'd listened to during the war and the newspaper articles that had given accounts of the battles, often mentioning those in the area who'd lost their lives in the line of duty. War was an ugly thing, but he knew it was a price that sometimes had to be paid in order to have freedom.

Dan's thoughts were halted when the telephone rang. Knowing it could be a client, he reached for the receiver. "Fisher's Photography Studio. Dan speaking."

"Hi, Danny. How are you this evening?" The lilting voice on the other end of the line purred like a kitten, and he recognized it immediately.

"I'm fine, Leona. How are you?"

"Okay." There was a brief pause. "You said you enjoyed my spaghetti and meatballs last week when you came over for supper, so I was hoping you'd join me tonight for my meat loaf special."

"I appreciate the offer, but I'm busy right now, Leona."

Dan's next-door neighbor's placating voice suddenly turned to ice. "I hope you're not giving me the brush-off."

"Of course not. I've got work to do in the studio, and I'll be here until quite late."

"I'm really disappointed, Danny."

Dan clenched the phone cord between his fingers. Leona Howard was a nice enough woman, but why did she have to be so pushy? "Can I take a rain check?" he asked.

"Okay, but I plan to collect on that rain check soon."

"I'd better get back to work, so I'll talk to you later. Goodbye, Leona." Dan hung up the phone with a sense of relief. He didn't want to hurt the woman's feelings, but they weren't right for each other. At least, she wasn't right for him. Leona was nothing like Darcy. In fact, she was the exact opposite of her. Leona usually wore her platinum blond hair in one of those wavy updos, with her bangs swept to one side. Darcy's chestnut-brown hair had been shoulder length and worn in a soft pageboy. Leona plastered on enough makeup to sink a battleship, and Darcy had worn hardly any at all.

Dan massaged his forehead, making little circles with the tips of his fingers. *Who am I kidding? I'm not ready to commit to another woman, and I may never be. Besides, Leona is not a Christian, and that fact alone would keep me from becoming seriously involved with her.*

A couple of times, when Leona first started inviting him to her house for a meal, Dan had asked her to attend church with him. She'd flatly refused, saying church was for weak people who needed a crutch. Leona wasn't weak, and she'd proved that when her husband was killed on the USS *Arizona* during the bombing of Pearl Harbor. Leona had become a nurse and picked up the pieces of her life so well that it made Dan wonder if she'd ever loved her husband at all.

A rumble in the pit of Dan's stomach reminded him that it was nearly suppertime. He momentarily fought the urge to call his wife on the phone and ask what she was fixing tonight. He glanced through the open door of his office, leading to the used-toy store on the other side of the building. There was

Darcy's quilt hanging over the wooden rack he'd made. The coverlet was a reminder of her undying love and brought him some measure of comfort.

Bev sank into a chair at the kitchen table and opened the newspaper. Yesterday had been her last day at Bethlehem Steel, and she hoped to find something else right away. She *needed* to, as the meager savings she'd put away wouldn't last long.

She scanned the HELP WANTED section but soon realized there were no bookkeeping jobs available. "They've probably all been taken by returning war veterans," she grumbled.

Her conscience pricked, and she bowed her head. "Forgive me, Lord. I'm thankful that so many of our soldiers have come home. I only wish Fred could have been one of them."

Tears stung Bev's eyes as she thought about the way her husband had been killed, along with thousands of other men and women who'd been at Pearl Harbor on December 7, 1941. For nearly four years now, Bev had been without Fred, but at least she'd had a job.

She returned her attention to the newspaper. Surely there had to be something she could do. She was about to give up and start supper when she noticed an ad she hadn't seen before.

Wanted: Reliable person to manage used-toy store. Must have good people skills and be able to balance the books. If interested, apply at Twice Loved, on the corner of North Main and Tenth Street, Easton, Pennsylvania.

She pursed her lips. "Maybe I should drop by there tomorrow after I take Amy to school. Even if I don't get the job, I might be able to find an inexpensive doll or stuffed animal I could put away for her Christmas present."

As if on cue, Bev's six-year-old daughter burst into the room. Her blue eyes brimmed with tears, and her chin trembled like a leaf caught in a breeze.

Bev reached out and pulled Amy into her arms. "What's wrong, honey?"

"I was playin' with Baby Sue, and her head fell off."

"Why don't you go get the doll, and I'll see if I can put her back together."

Amy shook her head as more tears came. "Her neck's tore. The head won't stay on."

Bev knew enough about rubber dolls to realize that once the body gave way, there was little that could be done except to buy a new doll.

Her gaze came to rest on the newspaper ad again. *I really do need to pay a visit to Twice Loved.*

CHAPTER 3

Bev stood in front of Twice Loved, studying the window display. There were several stuffed animals leaning against a stack of books, a toy fire truck, two cloth dolls, and a huge teddy bear with a red ribbon tied around its neck. Propped against the bear's feet was a sign that read: HELP WANTED. INQUIRE WITHIN.

Bev drew in a deep breath and pushed open the door. Inside, there was no one in sight, so she made her way to the wooden counter in the center of the room. A small bell sat on one end, and she gave it a jingle. A few minutes later, a door at the back of the store opened, and a man stepped out.

Her heart did a little flip-flop. He was tall with sandy-blond hair and wore a pair of tan slacks and a long-sleeved white shirt rolled up to the elbows.

Bev recognized him—but from where? She'd never been in this store before. She was tempted to ask if they'd met somewhere, but that might seem too forward.

The man stepped up beside her. "May I help you?"

Bev moistened her lips, feeling as though her tongue were tied in knots. "I—um—do you have any dolls?"

He smiled and made a sweeping gesture with his hand. "All over the store, plus toys of all sorts."

"I'm looking for something inexpensive that's in good condition."

"Shouldn't be a problem. Most of the toys are in pretty fair shape."

"Would you mind if I have a look around?"

"Help yourself." He stepped aside, and Bev walked slowly around the room until she came to a basket full of dolls. Surely there had to be something here Amy would like. And if they weren't too expensive, maybe she could buy two—one to replace Amy's Baby Sue, and the other for Amy's Christmas present.

Bev knelt in front of the basket and riffled through the dolls. A few minutes later, the man pulled up a short wooden stool and plunked down beside her. "Have we met before? You look familiar."

She felt the heat of a blush creep up the back of her neck. "I'm. . .uh. . .not sure. You look familiar to me, too."

They stared at one another a few seconds, and his scrutiny made Bev's cheeks grow even warmer. Suddenly she remembered where she'd seen the man. It was at Bethlehem Steel, the day she'd rushed into the hallway in tears after receiving her layoff notice. She had been mortified when she bumped the man's briefcase and it opened, spilling his photographs. But no, this couldn't be the same man. The man she'd met was obviously a photographer, not a used-toy salesman.

"I'm Dan Fisher, and I have a photography studio in the back of this building," he said, reaching out his hand.

"I'm Bev Winters." She was surprised by the firm yet gentle handshake he gave. "You're a photographer, not the owner of Twice Loved?"

"I do both. The used-toy store was my wife's business, and I took it over after she died two years ago from leukemia."

"I'm sorry for your loss." Bev's heart went out to Dan. It was plain to see from the way his hazel-colored eyes clouded over that he still missed his wife. She could understand that, for she missed Fred, too.

"Were you at Bethlehem Steel a few weeks ago?" she questioned.

He nodded. "I was asked to take some pictures for management, and—" Suddenly his face broke into a smile. "Say, you're that woman I bumped into, aren't you?"

"Actually, I think I bumped your briefcase."

"Ever since you came into the store, I've been trying to place you."

"Same here."

He motioned to the basket of dolls. "What kind of doll are you looking for?"

"I might buy two. One needs to be a baby doll, because my daughter's favorite doll is broken beyond repair. I'd also like to find something to give her for Christmas."

"How about this?" he said, pointing to a pretty doll with a bisque head.

Beth looked at the price tag and released a sigh. "I'm sure Amy would like it, but I can't afford that much right now." She plucked a baby doll from the basket. Its head was made from compressed wood, and the body was cloth. "I think this could replace Amy's rubber doll. How much is it? I don't see a price sticker."

"Some of the dolls in that basket came in last week, and I haven't had a chance to price them yet. How does twenty-five cents sound?"

Her mouth fell open. "You can't be serious. The doll probably cost at least three dollars when it was new."

He shrugged. "Maybe so, but it's used now, and twenty-five cents seems fair to me."

Bev sat a few seconds, thinking about his offer and trying to decide how best to reply. *I shouldn't have told him I couldn't afford the other doll. He probably feels sorry for me or thinks I'm a charity case.* She pinched the bridge of her nose, hoping to release some of the tension she felt. "Maybe I'll take this doll now. If I find a job soon, I might be able to purchase the bisque doll later."

His eyebrows lifted in obvious surprise. "You're not working at Bethlehem Steel any longer?"

She shook her head. "I was laid off. A returning soldier

used to have my bookkeeping position."

"I'm sorry." The compassion Bev saw in Dan's eyes made her want to cry, but she couldn't. It would be humiliating to break down in front of someone she barely knew.

"I understand that a lot of women who were filling job slots during the war are now out of work," he commented.

"Which would be fine if my husband were coming home."

"He was in the war?"

She nodded, willing her tears not to spill over. "Fred was killed during the Pearl Harbor attack. He was aboard the USS *Maryland*."

"I'm sorry," Dan said again. He reached out his hand as though he might touch her, but he quickly withdrew it and offered Bev a crooked grin instead.

She felt relief. One little sympathetic gesture and she might give in to her threatening tears.

"An elderly lady from church worked here part-time for a while," Dan said, as though needing to change the subject. "Alma fell and broke her hip a few weeks ago, so she had to quit. I've been trying to run both Darcy's toy store and my photo business ever since. It's become an almost impossible task, so I'm looking for someone to manage Twice Loved." He released a puff of air. "You think you might be interested in the job?"

Interested? Of course she was interested. That was one of the reasons she'd come here today. "I did notice your Help Wanted sign in the window," Bev admitted.

"I put it there yesterday. Also placed an ad in the newspaper."

"I read that ad in last night's paper," Bev said, feeling the need to be completely honest with him.

"You did?"

"Yes, but that's not the only reason I came here this morning. I really do need a doll for my daughter."

"I appreciate your truthfulness," he said with a smile. "I'm a Christian, and I believe honesty and integrity are important—especially where business matters are concerned."

"I'm a Christian, too." Bev fingered the lace edge on the baby doll's white nightgown. "I would have told you right away that I was interested in the job, but I was taken by surprise when you stepped into the room and I couldn't figure out where we had met."

He chuckled.

"So, about the position here. . .what hours would I be expected to work, and what would the job entail?"

"The store's closed on Sundays and Mondays, so I'd need you to work Tuesday through Saturday from nine to five. Could you manage that?"

Bev nibbled on the inside of her cheek as a sense of apprehension crept up her spine. Would he refuse to hire her if he knew she couldn't work Saturdays?

"Is there a problem?" he asked. "I sense some hesitation."

"The woman who watches my little girl after school is not available on weekends, so it would be difficult for me to work on Saturdays."

Dan shrugged. "That's not a problem. Bring your daughter to the store."

"You wouldn't mind?"

"Not at all. I have no children of my own, but I like kids." He shrugged. "Besides, a lot of kids come here with their folks. Maybe your daughter could keep them occupied while their parents shop. In between customers she can play with the toys."

Bev could hardly believe the man was so accommodating. Her boss at Bethlehem Steel would never have considered such a thing. Of course, there weren't a bunch of toys available there.

"What type of work would be expected of me?" she asked.

"Keeping the books, waiting on customers, going through boxes of toys that have been donated—that sort of thing."

"I think I could handle it." She felt her face heat up again. "That is, if you're willing to give me a try."

Dan stood and motioned her back to the counter.

Bev followed, wondering what he had in mind.

He reached underneath, pulled out a dark-green ledger, and flipped it open. "If you're a bookkeeper, you should be able to tell me if there's any hope for this store."

Bev peered at the page and frowned. The figures showed a decided lack of income, compared to the expenditures. "Why are so many of the toys given away for little or nothing?" she questioned.

"I donate a certain percentage of the proceeds from Twice Loved to children in need. It was something Darcy started before she died, and I plan to continue doing it." His forehead wrinkled. "So many kids had to do without during wartime."

"There have been so many people affected by the war—children who have lost a parent most of all." Bev drew in a deep breath and decided to ask the question uppermost on her mind. "How can you afford to pay me if the toy store operates in the red?"

"I make enough as a photographer to cover your wages." He motioned to the ledger. "And maybe you'll figure out a way to sell more toys and put Twice Loved in the black. My only concern is whether you'll be able to handle some of the repairs."

She lifted one eyebrow in question.

"The dirty toys that come in aren't such a problem. I usually take them home and soak them in the tub. However, I'm not good with a needle and thread, the way my wife was." Dan nodded toward a colorful patchwork quilt draped over a wooden rack on the opposite wall. "Darcy finished that shortly before she died."

Bev studied the item in question, taking in the vivid colors mixed with warm hues. "It's beautiful."

"Can you sew?" he asked.

She nodded. "I don't quilt, but I can mend. I've made most of Amy's and my clothes."

"Great. I think you'll do just fine."

"Is there anything else?"

He ran his fingers through the back of his hair, sending a spicy aroma into the air that tickled Bev's nose. "You know anything about electric trains?"

CHAPTER 4

On her trip home, Bev sat at the back of the bus, thinking about the job. Had she made a mistake in accepting Dan Fisher's invitation to work at Twice Loved? She was sure she could handle the books, because bookkeeping was something she had been doing for the last four years. But what did she know about fixing broken dolls and stuffed animals? And a toy train, of all things!

Bev winced. Had Dan been kidding about her repairing the broken train, or did he really expect her to tackle such a job? She would have asked about it right away, but he'd received a phone call that interrupted them. When he hung up, Bev paid for the baby doll, and not wanting to miss the next bus, she had left in a hurry and forgot to ask about the broken train.

She glanced at the small box lying in her lap. Amy's new doll. The one she'd paid a quarter for. She figured it was an act of charity, but since money was tight, she'd set her independent spirit aside.

I still can't believe he suggested that I bring Amy to the store. But tomorrow's Saturday, and I can't leave her alone. I hope things will go okay during my first day on the job.

"Excuse me, but is this seat taken?"

Bev was glad for the interruption, as her worrisome thoughts were taking her nowhere. "No, you're welcome to sit here," she said to the elderly woman who stood in the aisle.

The woman slid in next to her, pushing a strand of gray hair away from her eyes. "Whew! I almost missed the bus."

"I'm glad you made it." Bev could relate to what the woman had gone through. Since Bev didn't own a car, she usually rode the bus and had dashed for it many times when she'd been late. When she worked at Bethlehem Steel, which was several miles outside of town, Bev drove to work with a coworker who owned a Hudson and lived near her apartment. With her new job being downtown, though, she would ride the bus every day.

As the bus continued on its route, Bev watched the passing scenery—the Karldon Hotel, Easton City Hall, Maxwell's Book Store. How long had it been since she'd bought a new book to read? Money was tight, and America had begun rationing things during the war. She had a feeling that despite the end of the war some things might continue to be rationed for a while.

Even though Bev had Fred's monthly veteran's pension,

it was small and not enough to provide all the essentials she and Amy needed. Bev only wished her wages at Twice Loved wouldn't be coming from Dan's photography business. She hoped to find a way for the toy store to make more money and get out of the red, while keeping prices low.

Bev closed her eyes and leaned against the seat, willing herself to relax and give her troubles to the Lord. After all, He had provided her with a new job, and so quickly, too. She needed to trust Him and believe He would care for her and Amy in the days ahead.

Sometime later, Bev arrived at her apartment and was surprised to find a note taped to the door. She waited until she was inside to read it, dropping her coat and the box with the doll in it onto the couch. Then she took a seat and opened the folded paper.

Dear Mrs. Winters:

This is to inform you that due to the expected rise in heating costs this winter I need to raise your rent by five dollars a month. The increase will take effect on the fifteenth of October.

Thank you.

Sincerely,

Clyde Smithers, Manager

Bev moaned. This kind of news was not what she needed. The rent on her small two-bedroom apartment was already sixty dollars a month, and she didn't think she could afford another five. With the addition of bus fare to and from work every day, and the fact that her wages at Twice Loved wouldn't be as much as what she had made at Bethlehem Steel, she couldn't afford the rent increase.

Maybe I should look for an apartment closer to town so I can walk to work. That would save money, and perhaps I can find something cheaper to rent.

Bev dismissed that thought as quickly as it came. She had heard that apartments in the heart of the city were in demand, and with so many men and women returning from the war, it would be difficult to find one that wasn't already rented, let alone cheaper.

Bev massaged her pulsating forehead. Just when she thought the Lord was watching out for them, another problem had come along. Ever since Fred died, it seemed as if her whole world were out of control. Bev attended church on Sunday mornings, read her Bible regularly, and prayed every day. Yet her faith was beginning to waver.

Blinking back tears, she closed her eyes and prayed, "Lord, show me what to do about the increase in my rent. If there's something closer to town, please point the way."

For the last couple of hours, Dan had been sitting at his desk going over some paperwork. Trying to run two businesses by himself had put him behind in the photography studio. But that was about to change. Now that he'd hired Bev Winters to run Twice Loved, things would get back to normal. At least he hoped they would. What if Bev didn't work out? He didn't know much about the woman other than she had worked as a bookkeeper, had a young daughter, and was widowed. He hadn't thought to ask for a résumé or any references. He'd based his decision to hire Bev on her need for a job. That and the fact that she said she was a Christian.

A beautiful one at that, Dan thought, tapping his pencil along the edge of the desk. It wasn't just Bev's shiny dark hair and luminous blue eyes that attracted him either. There was something about her demeanor that reminded him of Darcy.

He rapped the side of his head with the pencil. "Get a grip on yourself. You hired the lady to run Twice Loved, not so you could become romantically involved."

The phone rang, and he grabbed for it, glad for the interruption. "Fisher's Photography. May I help you?"

"Hello, Dan. This is Pete Mackey, with *Family Life Magazine.* We talked at Bethlehem Steel a few weeks ago, remember?"

Dan's gaze went to the ceiling. "I hope you're not calling about that article you're doing on grief, because, as I told you before, I'm not interested in being interviewed."

"I'd hoped if you had a few weeks to think it over that you might have changed your mind."

"Nope. Sorry, Pete."

"Here's the phone number where I can be reached, just in case."

Dan studied a set of negatives on his desk as Pete rattled off his number. There was no point in writing it down because he had no intention of doing that interview.

"I appreciate your time," Pete said. "Please call if you ever want to talk."

"Okay, thanks. Good-bye, Pete."

Dan had no more than hung up the phone when he heard a knock on the door of his studio. *Wonder who it could be? I don't have any appointments scheduled for the rest of the day.*

When Dan opened the door, he discovered Leona Howard, holding a casserole dish wrapped in a towel with a paper sack balanced on top.

"Hi, Danny," she said, offering him a pleasant smile. "Since you've been too busy lately to have dinner at my place, I decided to bring a meal over to you this evening. It's Chicken Noodle Supreme."

Leona wore a maroon-colored, knee-length skirt with a single-breasted jacket that had wide lapels and padded shoulders. It looked like something a woman might wear when she went out to dinner—but not to drop off a casserole for a neighbor.

"I'm working right now," Dan said as she swept into the room, her fragrant perfume leaving a trail of roses behind.

"Surely you're ready for a break. I'll be disappointed if you don't try some of my yummy casserole." Leona nodded at the paper sack. "I even brought some dishes, silverware, and napkins, so all you need to provide is a place for me to set the table."

Dan was sure the woman wasn't going to take no for an answer, so he removed the negatives and paperwork from his desk and slipped them into a folder. "You can put the food here." He pulled out his desk chair, grabbed another one for Leona, and sat down.

She quickly set out the dishes, opened the lid of the casserole dish, and served them both a hefty amount. "Oh dear, I forgot to bring something to drink," she said with a frown. "Do you have anything cold on hand?"

He reached into the bottom drawer of his desk and grabbed a thermos. "It's coffee, so it's not cold."

She smiled. "That will be fine."

"Mind if I pray before we eat?"

She shrugged. "If it makes you feel better. I wasn't planning to poison you, Danny."

He bit back a chuckle. That thought had crossed his mind.

After the prayer, Dan poked his fork into the gooey mess she'd put on his plate and took a bite. Ugh! The stuff tasted worse than it looked. He grabbed his Thermos, twisted the lid, and gulped down some coffee.

Leona's lower lip protruded. "You don't like it?"

Searching for words that wouldn't be a lie, Dan mumbled, "It's. . .uh. . .different." He set the thermos lid down and wiped his mouth on the cloth napkin she had provided. "I'm really not hungry."

Leona pushed her chair aside, and it nearly toppled over. "I can tell you'd rather not eat it."

Dan opened his mouth to reassure her, but Leona gathered

her things so quickly that he barely had the presence of mind to say he was sorry.

"I'll try something different next time," she said as he followed her to the door. "Something I know you'll like."

CHAPTER 5

Dan took a swig of coffee and glanced at the clock on the far wall. Bev Winters should be here any minute and would be bringing her daughter along. He moved across the room and put the Open sign in the window. It was almost nine o'clock. Better to have the store ready for business on time, even if his new employee wasn't here yet.

I wonder if her bus was late, or maybe she had trouble getting her daughter out of bed. Sure hope I did the right thing in hiring her.

Dan thought about his favorite verse of scripture—2 Corinthians 1:3. It reminded him that God is our Comforter, and because He comforts in all our troubles, we should comfort those who have trouble as well. Through God's Word and the godly counsel of his pastor, Dan had been comforted many times since Darcy's death. It was only right that he should offer comfort to Bev, who was probably hurting from the loss of her husband and also her job. He'd known yesterday that he needed to give her a chance. If hiring her to work at Twice Loved could help them both during their time of need, then so much the better.

Dan's gaze came to rest on the clock again. It was now ten minutes after nine. Bev was late. Maybe she'd changed her mind about the job and wasn't coming.

The bell above the front door jingled, and his thoughts were halted. Bev entered the store holding a metal lunch pail in one hand and a brown pocketbook in the other. A young girl stood at her side, clutching the same doll he'd sold Bev yesterday afternoon.

"I'm sorry we're late." Bev patted the sides of her windblown hair and smoothed the wrinkles in her knee-length, navy-blue dress, covered by a short black jacket. "The bus was late, and there was more traffic this morning than I've seen in a long time."

"It's okay," Dan said with a nod. "There haven't been any customers yet." He smiled at the little girl who stood beside Bev. She was a beautiful child—curly black hair like her mother's, and the same brilliant blue eyes. She wore a beige-colored tweed coat with a pair of dark-green overalls with patched knees peeking out from underneath. "So, this must be Amy."

"Yes." Bev's generous smile seemed to light up the room.

Darcy used to smile like that, Dan noted.

"Amy, this is Mr. Fisher, and he owns this store where I'll be working."

The child smiled shyly and glanced around the shop. "I like it here."

"Me, too." Dan swallowed around the lump in his throat. He and Darcy had wanted children, but that wasn't to be. Did Bev Winters know how fortunate she was?

"Why don't you find a book to read?" Bev said to her daughter. "Mommy needs to begin working now."

Dan pointed across the room. "There's a table in the corner where you can sit if you want to read or work on a puzzle. Feel free to play with any of the toys that are in baskets sitting on the floor."

Amy didn't have to be asked twice. She slipped out of her coat and handed it to her mother. Then she sprinted across the room, grabbed a fat teddy bear from a wicker basket, and helped herself to a book from the bookcase. A few seconds later, she sat at the table wearing a contented grin.

Dan turned his attention back to Bev. "Should we take a look at some of the toys that need to be fixed?"

Her eyes widened. "Uh. . .about the toys. . ."

"What about them?"

"Yesterday you mentioned a broken train, and I thought I should let you know that I'm not the least bit mechanical."

He chuckled and led her over to the desk. "I was only kidding. The train will have to be sold as is."

A look of relief flooded her face. "There's an elderly man at my church who collects old trains. I could speak to him and see if he might be able to look at the broken train."

"That would be great."

Bev set her pocketbook and lunch pail on the desk, removed her jacket, and draped it and Amy's coat over the back of the wooden chair. "Which toys did you want me to see about fixing?"

"First, I'd like to tell you something."

"What's that?"

You're beautiful. Dan shook his head, hoping to clear his ridiculous thoughts. "Uh—the dress you're wearing might not be practical here at the store."

She crossed her arms. "Too dressy?"

"It's not that." Dan paused. How could he put this tactfully? "Sometimes you'll have to get down on the floor, in order to sort through the boxes of toys that come in. You'll also be working with glue and other repair items. It might be better if you wear slacks to work from now on."

She blinked. "You wouldn't mind?"

He shook his head.

"I was expected to wear a dress at Bethlehem Steel, so I figured—"

"Wear whatever you're comfortable in here, Bev. I trust you to use good judgment."

"Thank you, Mr. Fisher."

"Dan. Please call me Dan."

Bev's cheeks turned pink as something indefinable passed between them, and she looked quickly away. "Guess you'd better show me what to do, so I can get to work."

He glanced toward the room where his studio was located. "That makes two of us."

Bev's stomach growled as her gaze went to the clock on the wall across from her. It was almost noon, and she couldn't believe how quickly the morning had passed. She'd mended two doll dresses, stitched a stuffed kitten's eyes in place, and waited on several customers. In all that time, Amy had hardly made a peep. She'd kept herself occupied with various toys, books, and puzzles. Dan excused himself soon after showing Bev what needed to be done, and he'd been in his photography studio ever since.

Should I ask him to cover for me so I can see that Amy is fed, or should I serve Amy her lunch and try to eat my sandwich while I keep an eye out for customers? Guess the latter would be better, she decided. *No point bothering Dan. He's probably busy and might not appreciate the interruption. After all, he hired me so he could be free to operate his own business and not have to run back and forth between Twice Loved and the photography studio.*

"Amy, please have a seat at the table again, and I'll bring your lunch," Bev instructed her daughter, who was now on her knees in front of a stack of wooden blocks.

"Okay, Mommy." Amy lifted her baby doll by one arm. "Can Baby Sue eat lunch with me?"

Bev smiled, pleased that the child had accepted the new doll so readily and had even given it the same name as her old doll. "Sure, sweetie. Just don't give her anything to drink, all right?"

"Okay."

A few minutes later, Amy and Baby Sue were seated in the small wooden chairs opposite each other, a peanut butter and jelly sandwich and a cup of cold milk in front of Amy.

Bev said a quick prayer, thanking God for the food, then took her bologna sandwich and the remaining milk over to the desk so she could look at the ledger while she ate. From time to time she glanced up, wondering if or when Dan might emerge from his studio. But he didn't. The only evidence that he was in the back room was the occasional ringing of his telephone.

After lunch Bev encouraged Amy to lie on a piece of carpet next to the bookcase and take a nap. Amy slept with Baby Sue tucked under one arm and a stuffed elephant under the other.

Bev decided to use this quiet time to sort through some boxes she'd found in one corner of the room. She soon discovered they were full of Christmas decorations, and it put her in the mood to decorate the store for the holidays. Perhaps it was too soon for that though. It was early October, and most of the stores didn't set out their Christmas things until sometime in November. She set the box aside, planning to ask Dan if he would mind if she decorated Twice Loved a little early. If she put some Christmas items in the store window it might attract more customers. Besides, it would help Bev get into the spirit of the holiday season. For the past several Christmases, she'd forced herself to put up a tree. Christmas wasn't the same without Fred, but for Amy's sake, Bev had gone through the motions.

Pushing the decorations aside, she turned her attention to another box. This one was full of old train cars, reminding her that she should speak to Ellis Hampton when she saw him at church tomorrow morning. She hoped he would be willing to look at the broken train. It would be cute, set up in the store window under a small, decorated tree with several dolls and stuffed animals sitting off to one side.

Bev blinked back tears as a feeling of nostalgia washed over her. Christmas used to be such a happy time, first when she was a child growing up near the Pocono Mountains, and then after she'd married Fred and they moved to Easton.

She closed her eyes and thought about their last Christmas together. She could almost smell the fragrant scent of the cedar tree they'd cut down in the woods that year. Amy was only two, and Bev remembered the touching scene as Fred carried their daughter on his shoulders while they trudged through the snow. They'd laughed and thrown snowballs, eaten the chewy brownies Bev had made, and drank hot chocolate from the thermos she'd brought along.

Unwanted tears seeped under Bev's eyelashes and trickled down her cheeks. *Those happy days are gone for good.* Her mother and father had been killed in a car accident five years ago, and the ugly war had taken Fred away. It was hard not to feel bitter and become cynical when there were so many injustices in the world. But for Amy's sake, Beth was determined to make the best of her situation.

"Aha! I caught you sleeping on the job, didn't I?"

Bev jumped at the sound of Dan's deep voice.

"I—I wasn't sleeping." She sat up straight and swiped a hand across her damp cheeks.

"I was kidding about you taking a nap, but your daughter certainly is." Dan motioned across the room, where Amy lay curled on her side.

Bev nodded. "I suggested she rest awhile. I hope you don't mind."

"Why would I mind?"

She merely shrugged in reply. Dan didn't seem like the type to get upset over something like a child falling asleep inside his toy store. In fact, from the look on his face, Bev guessed he might be rather taken with her daughter.

Dan left the desk and headed across the room. When he reached the wooden rack where the colorful patchwork quilt was draped, he pulled it down. Turning to give Bev a quick smile, he moved over to where Amy lay sleeping. Then he bent at the waist, covered her with the quilt, and reached out to push a wayward curl off her forehead.

The sight was so touching that Bev's heart nearly melted. She barely knew Dan, yet she could tell he had a lot of love to give. How sad that he hadn't been blessed with any children of his own.

She swallowed around the lump in her throat. Why was life so unfair? Shouldn't only good things happen to good people?

CHAPTER 6

On Tuesday morning Bev showed up at Twice Loved wearing an olive green two-piece trouser suit, a pale yellow blouse, brown lace-up shoes, and the same jacket she'd worn on Saturday.

When Dan greeted her, she offered him a radiant smile. Then, as her fingers curled around the strap of her pocketbook, a little frown pinched her forehead. "I was wondering if it would be all right if I left the shop during my lunch hour today. There's an apartment for rent in the building two doors down, and I'd like the opportunity to look at it before it's taken."

"You're planning to move?"

She nodded. "My rent's going up to sixty-five dollars in a

few weeks, and since I live on the south side of town and have to catch the bus to get here, I thought if I could find something closer, it would be the wise thing to do."

Dan's heart went out to Bev. He could see by her troubled look that she was probably struggling financially. Many people had been faced with financial hardships during the war. "Mend and make do." That was the motto for the women in America. From the looks of the patches he'd seen on the knees of Amy's overalls the other day, Dan figured Bev had done her share of mending.

He rubbed his chin and contemplated a moment. "Maybe I can increase your wages."

Bev stared at the floor, twisting the purse strap back and forth. "Today's only my second day on the job, and I've done nothing to deserve a wage increase."

"I know, but—"

She held up her hand. "I don't need your charity, but I do need to look at that apartment today. Is it okay if I leave the store for an hour during lunch?"

"Sure, that'll be fine." Bev was obviously a proud woman, and he really couldn't fault her for that. Maybe he could find some other way to help.

"Thank you, Dan." She pursed her lips. "Well, I'd better get busy."

"Same here. I've got some phone calls to make."

She started across the room, but turned back around. "I almost forgot to ask. . . . Would you mind if I decorate the store window for Christmas a little early?"

Dan's eyebrows drew together. Other than attending the candlelight communion service at church on Christmas Eve, he hadn't done much to celebrate Christmas since Darcy died. His parents, who lived in Connecticut, had invited him to come to their place for the holidays, but Dan always turned them down, preferring to be alone.

He glanced around the store as bittersweet memories flooded over him like waves lapping against the Jersey shore. When Darcy was alive, she had decorated every nook and cranny of Twice Loved for the holidays.

"If you'd rather I wait until after Thanksgiving, I understand," Bev added. "I just thought it might bring in more customers if we had the window decorated a little sooner."

Dan tapped his foot against the hardwood floor. Would it hurt if the store were decorated? It didn't mean he would have to celebrate Christmas, and it wasn't as if he would be giving up memories of Darcy by allowing Bev to do something festive here. In fact, if Darcy were alive, he knew what she would do.

"Sure, go ahead. Do whatever you'd like with the store window," he conceded.

"I'll start on the decorations when I return from my lunch break," Bev said sweetly.

"Take as long as you need to look at that apartment. I'll be praying it's the right one."

"Thanks. I appreciate that."

Bev wanted to pinch herself. Not only was the apartment she

had looked at on Saturday within walking distance of Twice Loved, but the rent was five dollars cheaper than what she was paying now. Without hesitation she had signed the lease, and she hoped that by next weekend she and Amy would be in their new home.

The move would mean Amy had to change schools, but she was young and adjusted easily. It would solve the problem of her needing a babysitter after school, too, which meant one less expense. Since the closest elementary school was only a few blocks away, Amy could walk to Twice Loved after school on the days Bev was working. Of course, she knew she would have to check with Dan first and see if he approved of the idea.

Bev smiled as she pulled out the box of Christmas decorations. Everything was working out fine. She'd been worried for nothing.

For the next hour, Bev worked on the window decorations. She had spoken to Ellis Hampton after church yesterday, and he'd agreed to look at the broken train.

She knew it was too early to get a cut tree. She certainly didn't want it drying out and dropping needles everywhere.

For now, Bev hung several Christmas ornaments in the store window, along with some red and green bows. She also placed three dolls and a couple of stuffed animals in the center and included several small empty boxes, which were wrapped like Christmas presents.

It looks rather festive, she told herself as she stood off to one side and studied her work. She allowed herself a satisfied sigh and began humming the words to "White Christmas," swaying to the music.

"The window display looks great. Your humming's not so bad either."

Bev swiveled around. She hadn't realized Dan had come into the room and stood directly behind her. Her face flushed. "Thanks. I think it will look even better once the train is fixed and set up under a small tree." She chose not to mention her off-key music.

"Did you speak to that man from your church?" he asked, leaning against the inside casing of the window display and looking at her intently.

Bev nodded and moistened her lips. *Why do I feel so jittery whenever Dan's around?* "Ellis said he would come by sometime this afternoon," she said.

Dan smiled, but there was sadness in his hazel-colored eyes. Was he nostalgic about trains, or could something else be bothering him?

"I'll be anxious to hear what the train expert has to say." He took a few steps toward Bev but then backed away, jamming his hands into the pockets of his brown slacks. "I didn't get a chance to ask, since I was busy when you left last Saturday, but how'd things go with the apartment hunt?"

"It went well. If I can get some of the men from church to help transport my furniture, I'll be moving to my new place next Saturday. After I get off work here, of course."

"If you need the whole day to move, that won't be a problem. In fact, why don't we close the store that day, and I can help you?"

Bev noticed the look of compassion on Dan's face. Help her move? Was there no end to this man's charitable offers?

She opened her mouth to decline, but he interrupted her. "I can't get much into my Studebaker, but I know someone who has a pickup truck. I'm pretty sure I can borrow it."

"That's nice of you, but I really couldn't accept your help." Bev appreciated his generosity, but he'd already done enough by hiring her and allowing her to bring Amy to the shop on Saturdays.

He lifted his hand and leaned forward, almost touching her lips with his fingertips, but then he quickly lowered it. "I wish you'd reconsider."

Bev swallowed around the lump in her throat. Why was it that whenever anyone was nice to her, she felt all weepy and unable to express herself? She'd been that way since Fred was killed. And why was she so determined to do things on her own? Maybe she should accept Dan's help—just this once.

"Thanks," she murmured. "I appreciate your kindness."

His ears turned pink. "Just helping a friend."

CHAPTER 7

Bev closed the door behind a customer and glanced around the toy store. She couldn't believe she'd been working here three weeks already. So much had happened in that time—moving, getting Amy situated in her new school, and learning more about her job. She felt she was doing fairly well, for she'd sold twice as many toys in the last few days as she had the previous week. Working at Twice Loved was proving to be fun, with not nearly as much stress as her last job. No overbearing boss making unwanted advances either.

Bev had felt such relief when Dan agreed to let Amy come to the store after school. He even said having the child there might make some customers stay longer, since those who'd brought children along could shop at their leisure while Amy kept their little ones occupied.

There were times, like the Saturday Bev and Amy had moved, when Dan seemed so friendly and approachable. Other times he shut himself off, hiding behind the doors of his studio and barely saying more than a few words whenever he was around. Bev figured he was busy with pre-Christmas portraits, but it almost seemed as if he'd been avoiding her.

Have I done something wrong? she wondered. *Is he displeased with the way I do the books or how I run the store?*

She studied the room more closely. Everything looked neat and orderly. Cleaning and organizing was one of the first things she had done. She'd also placed some of the more interesting toys in strategic spots in order to catch the customer's attention when they entered the store. The Christmas decorations she'd put in the store window looked enticing, even though the train wasn't part of the display yet. Ellis had phoned yesterday, saying the train should be ready later this week and that he would bring it by.

Bev picked up the ledger from her desk and thumbed through the last few pages. Twice Loved was making more money than it had in several months—the profit column was proof of that.

So why did Dan seem so aloof? Was he dreading the holidays? If so, Bev couldn't blame him. This was the first year since Fred's death that she hadn't experienced anxiety about Christmas coming.

"It's probably because I'm working here among all these

toys," she said with a smile. "I feel like a kid again."

Bev closed the ledger and moved across the room to the sewing area. *Maybe I should invite Dan to join Amy and me for Thanksgiving dinner. It would be nice to have someone else to cook for. I could bake a small turkey, fix mashed potatoes, gravy, and stuffing. Maybe make a pumpkin and an apple pie.*

Bev took a seat at the sewing table and threaded her needle, prepared to mend the dress of the bisque doll she had chosen to give Amy for Christmas. Once the dress was repaired and the doll's wig combed and set in ringlets, she planned to put the doll in the storage closet at the back of the store until closer to Christmas. Then she would wrap it, take it home, and, when Amy wasn't looking, slip it under the tree she hoped to get for their new apartment.

Thinking of a tree caused Bev to reflect on the day they had moved. Her daughter's enthusiasm over the large living room with a tall ceiling was catching.

"We can have a giant Christmas tree, Mommy!" Amy had exclaimed. "Uncle Dan can help us decorate and climb the ladder to put the angel on top."

Bev didn't know what had prompted Amy to call Dan "Uncle," but he didn't seem to mind. In fact, the man had been patient and kind to Amy all during the move, even rocking her to sleep when she'd become tired and fussy that evening.

The bell above the door jingled, forcing Bev's thoughts aside. When Amy skipped into the room, Bev hurriedly slipped the doll's dress into a drawer.

"Mommy, Mommy, guess what?" Amy's cheeks were rosy,

and she was clearly out of breath.

"What is it, sweetie?" Bev asked, bending down to help her daughter out of her wool coat.

"No, I can't take my coat off yet," Amy said, thrusting out her lower lip.

"Why not?"

" 'Cause it's snowing, and I want to play in it!"

Bev glanced out the front window. Sure enough, silvery flakes fell from the sky like twinkling diamonds. And here it was only the second week of November.

"It's beautiful," she murmured.

"Can we build a snowman?" Amy's blue eyes glistened with excitement, as she wiggled from side to side.

"Simmer down," Bev said, giving her daughter a hug. "There's not nearly enough snow yet to make a snowball, let alone a snowman. If we had a place to build one, that is."

"We can put it out on the sidewalk in front of the store. I'll give it my hat and mittens to wear." Amy reached up to remove her stocking cap, but Bev stopped her.

"Whoa! You need your hat and mittens—you would get cold without them."

"What about the snowman? Won't he get cold without anything on his head or hands?"

Bev chuckled. "Oh Amy, I don't think—"

"What's all this about a snowman?"

Both Bev and Amy turned at the sound of Dan's deep voice. Then Amy darted across the room and grabbed hold of his hand. "It's snowing, Uncle Dan! Can we build a snowman?"

"Amy, I just told you there's not enough snow," Bev reminded her. "Besides, Uncle Dan—I mean, Mr. Fisher—is busy and doesn't have time to play in the snow."

Dan shook his head and gave Amy's hand a squeeze. "Who says I'm too busy to have a little fun?"

"Yippee!" Amy shouted.

Bev took a few steps toward him. "Do you really have the time for this?"

"For Amy and fun in the snow—absolutely!" His face sobered, and he bent down so he was eye level with the child. "There's not enough snow to build a snowman, but we can run up and down the sidewalk and catch snowflakes on our tongue." He glanced over at Bev and smiled. "How about it, Mommy? Why don't you slip into your coat and join us?"

She laughed self-consciously. "Oh I couldn't do that."

"Why not?"

She made a sweeping gesture with her hand. "Who would mind the store?"

Dan tweaked Amy's nose and gave Bev a quick wink. "Let the store mind itself, because I think we all deserve some fun!"

Dan couldn't remember when he'd felt so exuberant or enjoyed himself so much. Certainly not since Darcy had taken ill.

For the last half hour, the three of them had been running up and down the sidewalk, slipping and sliding in the icy snow, catching snowflakes on their tongues, and singing

Christmas carols at the top of their lungs. Some folks who passed by joined in their song. Some merely smiled and kept on walking. A few unfriendly faces shook their heads and mumbled something about it not being Christmas yet. One elderly woman glared at Dan and said, "Some people never grow up."

Dan didn't care what anyone thought. He'd been cooped up in his studio for several days and needed the fresh air. He drew in a deep breath, taking in a few snowflakes in the process. *If I had known this was going to feel so good, I would have done it sooner.*

The sidewalk was covered with a good inch of snow now, and feeling like a mischievous boy, Dan bent down and scooped up a handful of the powdery stuff. He then trotted up the sidewalk, grabbed hold of Bev's collar, and dropped the snow down the back of her coat.

She shrieked and whirled around. "Hey! That was cold!"

"Of course it's cold. Snow's always cold." Dan winked at Amy, and she snickered.

"Stop that, or I won't invite you to join Amy and me for Thanksgiving." Bev wrinkled her nose. "That is, if you have no other plans."

He grinned. "I have no plans, and I'd be happy to have dinner at your place."

Bev smiled, and Amy clapped her hands.

"Can I bring anything?"

She shook her head. "Just a hearty appetite."

Before Dan could respond, two teenage girls strode up to

them. Each held several wreaths in their hands. Dan recognized them and realized they attended his church.

"Hi, Mr. Fisher," Dorothy said. "Looks like you're havin' some fun today."

"Sure am," he replied with a smile.

"We came by to see if you'd like to buy a wreath for your front door," Amber put in.

He glanced at Bev. "Might be nice to have one hanging on the door of Twice Loved. What do you think?"

She nodded. "Sounds good to me."

Dorothy moved toward Bev. "Would you like to buy one to take home?"

"Thanks anyway, but it will be all I can do to afford a tree."

Dan was tempted to give Bev the money for a wreath, but he figured she would see it as charity. She'd made it clear that she didn't want his help and was making it difficult for him to do anything nice for her and Amy. So he kept quiet and paid the girls for one wreath, then went to hang it on the door of Twice Loved.

Just as the teens were leaving, an elderly couple showed up, wanting to buy something in the store.

"I'd better get back inside," Bev said, hurrying past Dan.

He nodded. "Amy and I will be there in a minute."

Bev and the couple entered the store, and Dan reached for Amy's hand. "How would you like to give your mother a special Christmas present this year?"

She grinned up at him with snowflakes melting on her dark, curly lashes. "What is it?"

"Can you keep a secret?"

She bobbed her head up and down.

"Let's go inside my photography studio, and I'll tell you about it."

CHAPTER 3

"I'm sorry, Leona," Dan said into the phone, "but I can't come to your place for Thanksgiving."

"Why not?"

"Because I've made other plans."

There was a long pause, and he could almost see Leona's furrowed brows.

"Are you going to spend the holiday with your folks this year?"

"No. I'll be staying in town."

"But you're having dinner with someone?"

Dan tapped his fingers along the edge of his desk, anxious to end this conversation. He still had some book work to do, and another photo shoot was scheduled in half an hour. "I've been invited to eat with Bev Winters and her daughter, Amy."

"Bev Winters? Who's she?" Leona's voice sounded strained, and Dan had a hunch she might be jealous. Of course, she had no right to be. He'd never given her any hope that he was interested in starting a relationship. Besides, Bev was an employee, not his girlfriend.

"Danny, are you still there?"

"Yes, Leona, although I do need to hang up. I've got a client coming soon."

"First tell me who this *Bev* person is."

"She's the woman I hired to run Twice Loved."

Leona made no reply.

"I really do need to go. Thanks for the invite."

Leona sighed. "Have a nice holiday, and I'll see you soon." She hung up the phone before he could say good-bye.

Dan massaged his forehead, feeling a headache coming on. He reached for his cup of lukewarm coffee and gulped some down as the picture of Darcy hanging on the far wall caught his attention. Even though it had been two years since her death, he still loved her and probably always would.

Bev had been scurrying around her apartment all morning, checking the turkey in the oven, dusting furniture, sweeping floors, setting the table, and preparing the rest of the meal. Amy was in the living room with her new coloring book and crayons. Last week, shortly after their romp in the snow, Bev had seen her daughter go into Dan's studio. When Amy emerged a short time later, she had a box of crayons and a coloring book, which she said were a gift from Dan.

Bev glanced at the clock on the far wall. It was one thirty. Dan should be here soon, and she still needed to change clothes and put on some makeup.

"I'll be in the bedroom getting ready!" Bev called to Amy. "If anyone knocks on the door, don't answer it. Come and get me, okay?"

"All right, Mommy."

A short time later, Bev stood in front of the small mirror hanging above her dresser. She'd chosen a dusty-pink rayon-crepe dress with inset sleeves to wear. It was homemade and last year's style, but she felt it looked presentable.

When Bev reached into her top dresser drawer for a pair of hose, she discovered that her one and only pair had a run in one leg that went all the way from the heel up to the top.

"I can't wear this," she muttered. "Maybe I should draw a line down the back of my leg, like I've seen some women do when they have no hosiery."

Bev rummaged around in her drawer until she found a dark-brown eyebrow pencil. Craning her neck, she stretched her left leg behind her and bent backwards. Beginning at the heel of her foot, she drew a line up past her knee and then did the same to the other leg. "That will have to do," she grumbled, wishing she had a full-length mirror so she could see how it looked.

A knock at the door let Bev know Dan had arrived. She clicked off the light and left the bedroom. When Bev opened the front door, she was surprised to see a wreath hanging there.

Dan smiled at her. “Happy Thanksgiving.”

“Same to you.” She pointed to the wreath. “This is pretty, but I told you not to bring anything except your appetite.”

He shrugged and turned his hands palm up. “It was there when I got here.”

Bev squinted at the item in question. It hadn’t been there this morning when she’d gone next door to borrow a cup of flour to make gravy.

“Looks like a mystery Santa Claus paid you a visit,” Dan said with a chuckle.

Bev had no idea who it could be, but the pretty wreath with a red bow did look festive, so she decided not to worry about who the donor was. She opened the door wider. “Please come inside.”

Dan sniffed the air as he entered Bev’s apartment. “Umm. . . something sure smells good.”

Bev nodded toward the kitchen. “That would be the turkey. Would you mind carving it for me?”

“I’d be happy to.”

“Follow me.”

Dan stopped at the living room to say hello to Amy, and then he caught up to Bev. When she’d opened the door to let him in, he had noticed how pretty she looked in her frilly pink dress. He hadn’t yet seen the backs of her legs, but now, as she led the way to the kitchen, Dan couldn’t help but notice the strange, squiggly dark lines running up both legs.

"What happened, Bev?" he queried. "Did Amy use her new crayons to draw on your legs?"

Bev whirled around, her face turning as pink as her dress. "I—I didn't have a decent pair of hose to wear, so I improvised."

Dan tried to keep a straight face, but he couldn't hold back the laughter bubbling in his throat.

Bev's eyes pooled with tears, and he realized he had embarrassed her. "I'm sorry. If you'd told me you needed new hosiery, I would have given you the money."

She lifted her chin. "I don't need your money or your pity, and I'm sorry you think my predicament is so funny."

"I don't really." He glanced at the crooked lines again and fought the temptation to gather her into his arms.

Bev craned her neck and stuck one leg out behind her. When she looked back at him, she wore a half smile. Soon the smile turned into a snicker. The snicker became a giggle, and the giggle turned into a chortle. She covered her mouth with the palm of her hand and stared up at him. "You had every right to laugh. What I did was pretty silly. But I was worried that if I didn't wear any hose, you'd think I wasn't properly dressed."

Dan shook his head. "I'd never think that, and as far as your being worried. . .I have a little quote about worry hanging in my studio."

"What does it say?"

" 'Worry is the darkroom in which negatives can develop.' "

She pursed her lips. "Your point is well taken. I do have a tendency to worry."

He wiggled his eyebrows. "Still want me to carve that bird?"

"Absolutely." She turned toward the door leading to the hallway. "While you do, I think I'll change into a comfortable pair of slacks."

"Good idea." Dan winked at Bev, and she scurried out of the room.

The rest of the afternoon went well, and Bev felt more relaxed wearing a pair of tan slacks and a cream-colored blouse than she had in the dress. After they'd stuffed themselves on turkey and all the trimmings, Bev, Dan, and Amy played a game of dominoes in the living room.

Soon Amy fell asleep, and Dan carried the child to her room. When he returned a few minutes later, he took a seat on the sofa beside Bev. She handed him a cup of coffee and placed two pieces of apple pie on the coffee table in front of them. It was pleasant sitting here with him. Bev hadn't felt this comfortable with a man since Fred was alive. Dan seemed so kind and compassionate, and he was a lot of fun. If she were looking for love and romance, it would be easy to fall for a man like him.

She glanced at Dan out of the corner of her eye. Was he experiencing the same feelings toward her? Had he enjoyed the day as much as she had?

As if he could read her thoughts, Dan reached over and took Bev's hand. "Thanks for inviting me today. I had a nice time, and the meal was delicious."

"You're welcome. I'm glad you came."

"I'd like to reciprocate," he said. "Would you and Amy go out to dinner with me some night next week?"

Bev moistened her lips, not sure how to respond. If she agreed to go to dinner, would that mean they were dating?

Of course not, silly. He just wants to say thank-you for today.

Bev leaned over and handed Dan his plate of apple pie. "A meal out sounds nice, but you're not obligated to—"

"I know that, Bev." He forked a piece of pie into his mouth. "Yum. Apple's my favorite."

"Thanks. My grandmother gave me the recipe."

They sat in companionable silence as they drank their coffee and ate the pie. When Dan finished, he set the empty plate and cup on the coffee table and stood. "Guess I should be going."

"Amy will be disappointed when she wakes up and finds you are gone."

He reached for his coat, which he'd placed on the back of a chair when he first arrived. "Tell your daughter I'll see her bright and early tomorrow. Since she has no school until Monday, you'll be bringing her to work with you, right?"

Bev nodded. "The day after Thanksgiving should be a busy time at the store."

"Which is why I plan to give you a hand, at least for part of the day."

"I appreciate that." Bev walked Dan to the door, and when

she opened it, he hesitated. She thought he might want to say something more, but he merely smiled and strolled into the hallway. “See you tomorrow, Bev.”

CHAPTER 9

Bev plugged in the lights on the small Christmas tree she and Amy had picked out this morning for Twice Loved, after Dan had given her some money to purchase it. Amy could decorate the tree with silver tinsel and shiny red glass balls, while Bev waited on customers.

The decorations would look even better if the toy train were here, Bev thought as she scrutinized the window display. *I wonder why Ellis hasn't come by yet. He was supposed to have it ready last week. If he doesn't show up soon, I may give him a call.*

"Isn't the tree pretty?" Amy asked, pulling Bev's thoughts aside.

"Yes, it's very nice. Now be sure to drape the strands of

tinsel neatly over the branches," Bev said as Amy dove into the box of decorations.

"I will."

The bell on the front door jingled, and Bev turned her head to see who had entered the store.

A young woman with platinum blond hair piled high on her head swept through the door holding a cardboard box in her hands. She wore a black wool coat with a fur collar, and a blue, knee-length skirt peeked out from underneath. The woman stood there a few seconds, fluttering her long lashes, as she glanced around the room.

"May I help you?" Bev asked.

"I came to see Danny. Is he here?"

Bev motioned toward the back room. "He's in his studio, but I believe he plans to work in the toy store later today. May I give him a message?"

The woman stared at Bev with a critical eye, and it made Bev feel uncomfortable. "Are you the person he hired to run Twice Loved?"

Bev nodded. "I'm Bev Winters. Are you a friend of Dan's, or are you here looking for a used toy?"

"My name's Leona Howard. I'm Danny's neighbor and a good friend." She tapped her long red fingernails along the edge of the box. "I have no need for used toys, but I would like you to tell Danny I'm here and wish to speak with him."

Bev glanced at the back room again. "I believe he's on the phone, and I would hate to interrupt him. So if you'd like to wait—"

"Fine. I'll get him myself." Leona pushed past Bev, bumping her arm with the box.

"I—I really don't think—"

"Just go back to whatever you were doing!" Leona called over her shoulder.

Bev stood there dumbfounded as the brazen woman entered Dan's studio without even knocking. Then with a shrug, she took a seat at the desk, knowing she needed to make price stickers for some newly donated stuffed animals and get them set out.

Some time later, the door to Dan's studio opened. Leona and Dan stepped into the hall.

"Thanks for the pumpkin pie, Leona."

"Now don't forget that rain check you promised me, Danny," Leona said sweetly. "How about one night next week?"

Bev put her head down and forced herself to focus on the project before her. It wasn't her nature to eavesdrop, but it was hard to think about anything other than Dan and his lady friend. She glanced up once, and it was just in time to see Leona kiss Dan on the cheek. He grinned kind of self-consciously, and his ears turned red.

That's what you get for thinking you might have a chance with Dan, Bev fumed. Was that what she believed? Could she and Dan have a relationship that went beyond boss to employee, or friend to friend? Probably not, if he was dating his flamboyant neighbor. Besides, after Fred died, Bev had decided that she didn't need another man in her life. It would be easier on her emotions if she could learn to manage on her own. Of course, the absence of romantic love had left a huge void in her life.

Dan walked Leona to the front door, glancing at Bev as he passed. She averted her gaze and tried to concentrate on the price stickers in front of her.

"See you soon, Danny," Leona said, reaching for the doorknob. The door swung open before she could turn the knob, and in walked Ellis Hampton with a large box.

"I've brought the train," he announced.

Glad for the interruption, Bev pushed her chair away from the desk. "Oh good. I'm happy you came by today, Ellis."

"I'm sorry it took me so long to get the engine repaired, but I ran into a few problems," he apologized.

"That's all right. Let's get it set up under the tree in the display window." Bev was almost at Ellis's side when Leona took a step backwards. The two women collided, and Leona collapsed on the floor.

CHAPTER 10

"Are you all right?" Dan knelt next to Leona, who appeared to be more embarrassed than anything else.

"I–I'm fine," she stammered, "but I think the heel of my shoe is broken." She pulled off her shoe and held it up for his inspection.

"Yep. The heel's almost off." He helped Leona to her feet. "Maybe I can put some glue on it to help hold it together until you can get the shoe properly repaired."

She glared at Bev. "This is all your fault. If you hadn't gotten in my way, I never would have fallen."

Bev's cheeks were pink, and she looked visibly shaken. "I–I'm sorry, but I wasn't expecting you to step backward."

Leona's face contorted. "So now it's my fault?"

"I didn't say that. I just meant—"

Dan stepped between the two women. "It was only an accident, but if it will make you feel better, Leona, I'll pay for the repair of your shoe."

"Thank you, Danny. I appreciate that." She batted her eyelashes at him.

"I'm glad you weren't hurt, and I'm sorry we bumped into each other." Bev reached her hand out to Leona, but the woman moved quickly away. She turned with a shrug and followed Ellis to the window display, where Amy was decorating the tree.

Leona removed her other shoe and handed it to Dan. "It might be a good idea if you check this one over, too."

He led the way to his studio and, once they were inside, motioned to the chair beside his desk. "Have a seat, and I'll see if I can find some glue."

Leona dropped into the chair with a groan. "That woman you hired is sure a pain."

Dan looked up from the desk drawer he was rummaging through. "What's that supposed to mean?"

"When I first came into the store, she wouldn't even let me talk to you. Said something about you being on the phone. Then after I told her I was going to your studio anyway, she tried to stop me." Leona frowned. "I think she's jealous because I'm prettier than she is. That's probably why she tripped me."

Dan blew out a ragged breath. "I'm sure she wasn't trying to trip you, Leona. Bev's a nice lady."

"How would you know that? She's only been working for you a short time."

He squeezed a layer of glue onto the broken heel and gave no reply.

"Are you dating the woman? Is that why you've been giving me the brush-off lately?"

He squinted. "What? No!"

She smiled. "That's good news, because I wouldn't like it if you were interested in some other woman. I think we—"

Dan handed her the shoe. "Here. I believe this will hold until you get home."

"Thanks."

He leaned forward with both elbows on his desk. "Leona, I think I need to clarify a few things."

She blinked and gave him another charming smile. "What things?"

He cleared his throat, searching for words that wouldn't sound hurtful. "I'm not completely over my wife's death yet, so there's no chance of me becoming romantically interested in anyone right now."

Leona opened her mouth, but he held up his hand. "Please, hear me out."

She clamped her lips tightly together and sat there with her arms folded.

Dan reached inside another drawer and retrieved his Bible. When he placed it on the desk, she frowned. "What's that for?"

"I'm a Christian, Leona. I believe God sent His Son to die for my sins."

She shook her head. “Oh no, Danny. You’re too nice to have ever sinned.”

“That’s not true. Romans 3:23 says, ‘For all have sinned, and come short of the glory of God.’”

“Are you saying that includes me? Do you think I’m a sinner, Danny?”

“We all are,” he answered. “Everyone needs to find forgiveness for his or her sins, and the only way is through Jesus Christ.”

“I’ll have you know I did a lot of volunteer work during the war, in addition to my nursing duties,” she said with a huff. “I’ve always tried to be a good person, so I don’t need anyone telling me I’m a sinner.”

“I’m sorry you feel that way.”

Leona wrinkled her nose. “And I don’t see what any of this has to do with you and me developing a relationship.” She relaxed her face and reached over to touch his arm. “I can make you forget about the pain of losing your wife if you’ll give me half a chance.”

“The Bible teaches that those who believe in Jesus should not be unequally yoked with unbelievers, Leona. So even if I were ready to begin a relationship, it would have to be with a woman who believes in Christ as I do.”

Her face flamed. “You mean because I don’t go to church and rub elbows with a bunch of hypocrites, I’m not good enough for you?”

“That’s not what I’m saying.”

“What, then?”

Lord, help me, Dan prayed. His fingers traced the cover of the Bible. "As a Christian, I know it wouldn't be right to date someone who doesn't share my beliefs."

"What about that woman you spent Thanksgiving with?"

"What about her?"

"Does she go to church and believe in the same religious things as you?"

Dan closed his eyes as a mental picture of Bev flashed into his mind. She was a Christian, and as near as he could tell, she lived like one. Ever since he'd first met Bev, he'd been attracted to her sweet, caring disposition. She reminded him of Darcy in so many ways. He rubbed the bridge of his nose. *If that's so, then why can't I—*

Leona shook his arm, and Dan's eyes popped open. "Are you ignoring me?"

"No, but I. . ."

She pursed her lips. "I want to know one thing before I go."

"What's that?"

"If you have no interest in me, then why have you been leading me on?"

Dan cringed. Had he led Leona on? He'd thought he was being kind and neighborly when he'd agreed to have dinner with her a few times. He was only trying to set a Christian example.

"If I led you on, I'm sorry," he said.

Leona stood and pushed her chair aside with such force it nearly toppled to the floor. She grabbed her shoes and tromped across the room, but before she reached the door, she whirled around. "Just so you know—you're not the only fish in the Atlantic Ocean. When you turned me down for Thanksgiving dinner, I invited an old army buddy of my husband's over, and he was more than willing to share the meal with me."

Dan was about to comment when she added, "I'll send you the bill for the shoe repairs!" The door clicked shut, and Leona was gone.

Dan leaned forward and continued to rub the pulsating spot on his forehead. *I never should have had dinner with her.* When he glanced at the picture of Darcy, he thought of Bev again, and feelings of confusion swirled around in his brain like a frightening hurricane.

"Come look at what I found, Mommy!" Amy called to Bev.

Several minutes ago, the child had become bored with decorating the tree and had wandered over to a box of stuffed toys that had recently been donated to Twice Loved.

"I'm busy, honey. Can it wait awhile?" Bev asked over her shoulder. She and Ellis were still trying to get the train set up.

"That's okay. I can manage on my own if you need to see what your daughter wants," Ellis said with a grin. "I've got six grandkids, and I know how it is when one of 'em gets excited about something."

Bev smiled gratefully. "Thanks. I'll be back soon." She stepped across the room and knelt on the floor beside Amy. "Let's see what you've found."

Amy lifted a bedraggled-looking teddy bear from the box and gave it a hug. "He reminds me of Uncle Dan."

Bev tipped her head and studied the bear. One eye was missing, both paws were torn, the blue ribbon around its neck was faded, and some of the fur on the bear's stomach was gone. He didn't look anything like Dan, who was always nicely dressed, with his hair combed just right.

"What is there about the bear that makes you think of Dan?" Bev asked her daughter.

"He needs someone to fix him, Mommy," Amy said in a serious tone. "I think he's lonely and has no one to love." She pointed to the bear. "Can we take him home so he won't be sad?"

Bev's eyes stung with unshed tears. She didn't know why she felt like crying. Was it the touching scene with Amy and the bear, or did she feel sorry for herself because, like the tattered bear, she too was lonely and needed love? Was it possible that Dan felt that way, too?

"I'll tell you what," Bev said, giving Amy's arm a gentle squeeze. "If you promise to help me finish decorating the tree in the window, I'll see about buying that bear for you."

"Can he go home with us today?"

"Yes. After I patch him up."

"Okay, but I would love the bear just the way he is."

Bev smiled. "That's how Jesus sees us, and the best part is that He loves us the way we are." She held out her hand. "Should we go back to the window and finish the tree now?"

Amy nodded and grabbed the bear by one torn paw. "Until

we're ready to go home, I'm gonna put him in the window with the dolls and stuffed toys. That way he can see all the people who walk by the store."

As Bev started across the room, the door to Dan's photography studio opened. Leona marched through the toy store with a pained expression on her face.

Bev was tempted to say something, but the woman's angry glare made her decide to keep quiet.

A few seconds after Leona stormed out of the store, Dan emerged from his studio, wearing his coat, hat, and a pair of gloves. He looked upset, too. Was he mad at Bev for bumping into his girlfriend? Did he think she had done it on purpose?

"I'm sorry, but something's come up and I won't be able to help you today after all." He nodded at Bev.

"I'm sure I can manage."

He was almost to the door, when he halted. "Uh—can we take a rain check on that dinner I promised you and Amy?"

She swallowed around the lump in her throat. "Sure. It's probably best if we don't go out anyway."

Dan merely shrugged and opened the door.

He's probably going after Leona. Bev reached into the cardboard box and removed the train's caboose. She was on the verge of tears. What had happened between yesterday's pleasant Thanksgiving dinner and today? *It must be Leona Howard.*

At that moment, Bev made a decision. From this point on, there would be no more romps in the snow or friendly dinners. Her relationship with her boss must be kept strictly business.

CHAPTER 11

Holding tightly to Amy's hand, Bev trudged up the stairs to her apartment. Today was Thursday, and her workweek was nearly finished. The last two weeks had been the hardest she had experienced since Dan hired her to run Twice Loved. Not only had there been more customers than usual, but despite her best intentions, she continued to struggle with her feelings for Dan. He seemed sweet and attentive where Amy was concerned, even allowing her to visit his photography studio a couple of times. He'd also taken the child Christmas shopping one afternoon, which gave Bev the freedom to wait on customers without any distractions. Around Bev, however, Dan was distant and appeared to be preoccupied. He'd been friendly and attentive until the day after Thanksgiving, and

Bev didn't know what had happened to change things.

She'd thought at first that Dan's lack of interest in her was due to Leona Howard, but shortly after the woman's last visit to the store, Dan had told Bev he had informed Leona he wasn't free to pursue a relationship with her because she wasn't a Christian. He'd also made it clear that he hadn't fully recovered from his wife's death and didn't know if he would ever be ready for a relationship with another woman.

Bev opened the door to her apartment, allowing her thoughts to return to the present. She and Amy had purchased a Christmas tree at a reduced price, and the man at the tree lot would be delivering it soon. For the rest of the evening, she planned for the two of them to decorate the tree, snack on popcorn and apple cider, and sing whatever Christmas songs were played on the radio.

That should take my mind off Dan Fisher, Bev told herself as she entered the living room and clicked on the light.

Amy went straight to her room and returned a few minutes later with Baby Sue. She placed the doll on the sofa and plunked down beside her. "We're gonna wait right here till the tree arrives," she announced.

"I think it's here already, because I hear the rumbling of a truck."

Amy jumped up and raced for the door. Bev caught her hand, and the two of them hurried down the steps and onto the sidewalk.

The delivery man was already unloading the tree from the back of his pickup. "Want me to haul this upstairs for you?"

Bev shook her head. "I'm sure I can manage."

"It's a pretty big tree, ma'am."

"Thanks anyway."

He merely shrugged and climbed back into his truck.

Grabbing hold of the cumbersome tree trunk and directing Amy to go ahead of her, Bev huffed and puffed her way up the flight of stairs until she stood in front of her door. She leaned the tree against the wall and studied it, wondering if the oversize tree could be squeezed through the doorway.

She turned to Amy. "Sweetie, I want you to go into the living room and wait for me. After I bring the tree inside, we can begin decorating it."

"Okay."

Amy disappeared inside, and Bev grabbed hold of the tree, lining the trunk up with the door. She gave it a hefty thrust, but it only went halfway and wedged against the doorjamb. *"Oomph!"* She pushed hard again, almost losing her balance and catching herself before she fell into the scraggly branches.

Bev dropped to her knees and crawled under the limbs. *Maybe I can grab hold of the trunk and push it through that way.* Grasping both sides, she gritted her teeth and gave it a shove. The tree didn't budge.

With a sense of determination, Bev reassessed her situation. This time, facing the hallway, she would back in under the branches, grab hold, and try to pull the tree as she scooted through the doorway.

Bev had backed partway through the evergreen tunnel when a pair of men's shoes appeared. She froze.

The branches above her head parted, and Dan grinned down at her. "Oops. Looks like I'm too late."

"Too late for what?"

"I. . .uh. . .brought you a tree."

"You did what?"

He shuffled his feet a few times, and Bev pushed against the branches of the tree again, hoping to dislodge it. In the process, her hair stuck to a prickly bough. "I'm trapped, and so is the tree," she admitted sheepishly.

Dan reached through and untangled her hair. "See if you can back your way into the living room, and I'll try to follow with the tree."

Bev was skeptical but did as he suggested. Once she had clambered out from under the branches, she stood off to one side and waited to see what would happen.

To her amazement, Dan and the tree made their entrance a few minutes later. He obviously had more strength than she did.

After Amy greeted "Uncle Dan," Bev asked the child to go to her room and play. Then she turned to face Dan. "Now what's this about you bringing another tree?"

He swiped his hand across his damp forehead. "I—I figured you probably couldn't afford to buy a nice tree, so I bought you one and was going to leave it outside your door."

"An anonymous gift?"

He nodded and offered her a sheepish grin. "To be perfectly honest, I've done a couple other secret things, too."

She frowned. "Such as?"

He pointed to the front door. "While I wasn't the one who actually hung the wreath there, I did pay for it and asked the girls from church to put it on your door Thanksgiving morning."

Bev sank onto the couch. "Anything else I should know?"

He shifted uneasily. "Well. . ."

She blew out an exasperated breath.

"I know the man who owns this building, and when you said you were interested in renting an apartment here but might not be able to afford it, I agreed to pay your landlord the extra twenty dollars he normally would have charged per month."

Bev's mouth fell open. "Why would you do such a thing without asking me?"

"When I offered to increase your wages, you flatly refused, and several times you've mentioned that you don't want any charity. I thought the only way I could help was to do it anonymously."

Bev's body trembled as she fought for control. How dare this man go behind her back! "Please take the tree and the wreath to your own home. I'll speak to Mr. Dawson in the morning about the rent."

"Does that mean you won't accept any of my gifts?"

She shook her head as tears pooled in her eyes.

"I'm sorry if I've offended you, Bev."

She made no reply.

"I–I'd better get going." Dan turned for the door. "I hope I'll see you at the store tomorrow."

As much as she was tempted to quit working at Twice

Loved, Bev knew it would be difficult to find another job. Besides, she enjoyed the work she did there. "I'll make sure I'm on time," she mumbled.

The following morning, Bev found it difficult to concentrate on her work. Last night, she and Amy had decorated their tree, and she'd lain awake for hours thinking about Dan and the gifts he'd given her in secret. She had lost her temper and hadn't shown any appreciation for his thoughtfulness. *I need to apologize, but he also has to understand that I won't accept his charity.*

She glanced around thc store. Christmas was only a few days away, and most of the toys had been picked over. Most that werc left needed repair. She'd been too busy with customers to get more mending done. She was also behind on the bookwork and wanted to finish that before the week was out. It was time to get busy and quit thinking about Dan.

Since there were no customers at the moment, Bev decided to start with the book work. She seated herself at the desk, opened the drawer, and reached for the ledger, prepared to record the previous day's receipts.

Near the back of the drawer, she discovered a folded slip of paper. Funny, she'd never noticed it before. Curious, she unfolded the paper and silently read the words.

One thing I have learned since I was diagnosed with leukemia is not to worry about things I can't change. Every day God gives me is like a special gift, and I am putting my trust in Him. I've also learned to accept help whenever it's offered. I used to be too proud to ask for assistance, thinking I could do everything in my own strength. But since I became sick, I have no choice except to rely on others. Dan has been especially helpful, often setting his own needs aside for mine. I know he would rather be in his photography studio than at the toy store, yet he works here without complaint.

Bev blinked away tears. Dan's late wife had obviously written the note before she'd become too ill to be at the store, but for whom was it intended? Perhaps it was a letter to a friend or family member and Darcy had forgotten to mail it.

The poor woman had been through more than Bev could imagine, yet Bev realized Darcy had kept a positive, thankful attitude despite her ill health. She'd learned not to worry and had been willing to accept help, two areas in which Bev often struggled.

She realized, too, that Dan had only been trying to help when he'd given money toward her rent and purchased the tree and wreath. Even so, she didn't want to feel beholden to a man who only saw her as his employee—a man who was still in love with his wife and might never be ready for a relationship with another woman. Too bad she hadn't been able to keep from falling in love with him.

Dan stared at Darcy's Bible lying on his desk. He'd discovered it in the bottom drawer of their dresser this morning and felt compelled to bring it to work with him. Maybe it was because Christmas was fast approaching and he needed the comfort of having something near that belonged to his wife. This was Darcy's favorite time of the year, and every Christmas carol he heard on the radio, every decorated tree he saw in a window, and each Christmas shopper who came into the toy store reminded him of her.

Dan leaned forward and closed his eyes. *Help me, Lord. Help me not to forget my sweet Darcy.*

He had been fighting his attraction to Bev ever since she came into the store looking for a doll for her daughter, yet he hadn't succumbed to the temptation of telling her how he felt. He couldn't. It wouldn't be fair to his wife's memory.

Dan opened his eyes and randomly turned the pages of Darcy's Bible. To his surprise, an envelope fell out, and he saw that it was addressed to him. With trembling fingers, he tore open the flap and removed the piece of paper.

My Dearest Dan,

If you're reading this letter, then I have passed from this world into the next. One thing you can be sure of is that I'm no longer in pain. Take comfort in knowing I am healed and in my Savior's arms.

Dan's throat constricted as he tried to imagine his precious wife running through the streets of heaven, whole and at peace. With a need to know what else she had written, he read on.

My greatest concern is that you will continue to grieve after I'm gone, when you should be moving on with your life. You're a wonderful Christian man who has so much love and compassion to give. Please don't spend excessive time mourning for me. Praise God that I'm happy, and ask Him to bring joy into your life again.

Just as you and I have shared the love of Jesus with others, I pray you will continue to do the same—not only through what we've done at Twice Loved but in your personal relationships.

It's my prayer that God will bring you a special Christian lady, because I know you will be the same wonderful husband to her as you have been to me.

As you know, I always wanted to give you children, and I pray the Lord will bless you and your new wife with a family. Please know that by loving and being loved in return you will be honoring my wishes.

May God richly bless you in the days to come.

All my love,
Darcy

Tears welled up in Dan's eyes and spilled onto his cheeks. Darcy's letter was like healing balm, given at just the right time. He realized now that Darcy wanted him to be happy and to find love again. But could he find it with Bev? Was she the one God meant for him? If so, then he had some fences to mend.

Dan reached for the telephone. "First things first."

"*Family Life Magazine*," a woman answered on the second ring.

"May I speak to Pete Mackey?"

"One moment, please, and I'll see if he's in."

There was a brief pause, then, "Mackey here."

"Pete, this is Dan Fisher, with Fisher Photography."

"Ah yes, I remember. How are you, Dan?"

"I'm doing okay. Listen, Pete, I was wondering if you're still interested in interviewing me for that article you're writing on grief."

"Sure am. When can we talk?"

"I'll give you a call right after the New Year. How does that sound?"

"Great! Thanks, Dan. I'm glad you've changed your mind."

Dan smiled. "Actually, it was my late wife who changed my mind, but I'll tell you about that during the interview."

"Okay. I'll look forward to hearing from you."

Dan hung up the phone feeling as if a heavy weight had been lifted from his shoulders. Now he had one more hurdle to jump, and that *couldn't* wait until after the New Year. He pushed his chair away from the desk and headed down the hall for Twice Loved.

When he entered the store, he realized Bev was with a customer. He paused inside the door, waiting for her to finish wrapping a doll for an elderly gentleman. As soon as the man left, Dan stepped up to her. "If you have a minute, I'd like to speak with you."

She tipped her head. "Is something wrong?"

"Not unless you—"

The telephone rang, interrupting him.

"I'd better get that." Bev moved to the desk and picked up the receiver. "Twice Loved. May I help you?" Her face paled, and Dan felt immediate concern. "Thank you for letting me know. I'll be right there."

"What's wrong?" he asked when she hung up the phone.

Bev turned to face him, her eyes pooling with tears. "That was Amy's teacher. Amy fell from a swing during recess and has been taken to the hospital."

CHAPTER 12

Bev paced the floor of the hospital waiting room, anxious for some word on her daughter's condition.

"You're going to wear a hole in the linoleum. Please come sit beside me and try to relax," Dan said, patting the chair next to him.

She clenched her fingers and continued to walk back and forth in front of the window. "What if her leg's broken or she has a concussion? What if—"

Dan left his seat and came to stand beside her. "Whatever is wrong, we'll get through it together."

We? After the way I spoke to him last night, why is Dan being so nice? And what does he mean when he says "we"? Bev glanced at him out of the corner of her eye.

"It's going to be okay," he said with the voice of assurance. "Amy's a tough little girl, and she's got youth on her side."

Bev nodded slowly. "I know, but—"

"But you're her mother, and you have a tendency to worry."

"Yes."

"I understand, but worry won't change a thing." He took Bev's hand and led her over to the chairs. "Let's pray, shall we?"

Bev glanced around the room. There was an elderly couple sitting across from them, but they seemed to be engrossed in their magazines. "You want to pray now?"

Dan offered her a reassuring smile. "Absolutely." In a quiet voice, he prayed, "Heavenly Father, we ask You to be with Amy and calm her if she's frightened. Give the doctors wisdom in their diagnosis, and help Bev remember to cast her burdens on You, the Great Physician."

Bev thought of a verse of scripture from the book of Matthew she had read the other evening. " 'Take therefore no thought for the morrow: for the morrow shall take thought for the things of itself.' "

Lately, she'd been trying not to worry so much, but staying calm was hard to do when something went wrong. Especially when that "something" concerned her daughter.

A few minutes later, a nurse entered the room and called to Bev. "The tests are done, and you may see your daughter now."

"Are her injuries serious?" Bev tried to keep her voice calm, but her insides churned like an eggbeater.

"The doctor will give you the details," the nurse replied, "but Amy's going to be fine."

Bev drew in a deep breath. *Thank You, Jesus.* She turned to Dan. "Would you like to come with me?"

He nodded and took her hand.

Dan stood at the foot of Amy's bed, relief flooding his soul. Her leg wasn't broken, but her ankle had been badly sprained. She did have a concussion, though it was thought to be mild. The doctor wanted to keep her overnight for observation.

Bev sat in the chair beside Amy, holding her hand and murmuring words of comfort. It was a touching scene, and Dan felt like an intruder.

Maybe I should leave the two of them alone.

He turned toward the door, but Amy called out to him. "Where ya goin', Uncle Dan?"

"To the waiting room so you and your mother can talk."

Amy looked over at Bev. "We want Uncle Dan here, don't we, Mommy?"

Bev nodded. "If he wants to be."

Dan rushed to the side of the bed and stood behind Bev's chair. "Of course I want to be. I want. . ." What exactly did he want? Was it to marry Bev and help her raise Amy? He rubbed the bridge of his nose. No, it was too soon for that. They'd only known each other a few months.

"Can you come to our place for Christmas dinner, like you did on Thanksgiving?" the child asked.

Dan's gaze went to Bev, seeking her approval—or at least hoping for a clue as to whether she wanted him there or not.

She smiled. "I'm sorry for the unkind things I said when you stopped by our place with the tree."

"It's okay. I understand."

"No. I was wrong to refuse your help and the offer of gifts, and I hope you'll accept my apology."

"Only if you will accept mine for overstepping my boundaries."

She nodded. "If you have no other plans for Christmas, we'd love to have you join us."

He shook his head. "I don't think coming to your place is a good idea."

Tears welled up in Amy's eyes, and her lower lip trembled. "Why not? We had fun on Thanksgiving, didn't we, Uncle Dan?"

Dan felt immediate regret for his poor choice of words. Leaning over the bed, he took the child's other hand. "I had a wonderful time on Thanksgiving. It was the best day I've had in a long time."

"Then why won't you come for Christmas?" This question came from Bev, whose vivid blue eyes were full of questions.

He smiled. "Because I'd like to have you and Amy over to my house for Christmas dinner."

Bev's mouth dropped open. "You're planning to cook the meal?"

He shrugged. "Sure, why not?"

Amy giggled. "Can ya make pumpkin pies?"

Dan grinned then winked at Bev. "Actually, I was hoping you might furnish the pies, but I can roast the turkey and fix the rest of the dinner."

Bev's expression was dubious at first, but she gave him a nod. "It's a deal."

Dan had been rushing around for hours, checking on the bird he'd put in the oven early this morning, peeling and cutting the potatoes and carrots he planned to boil later on and placing presents under the tree. He wanted everything to be perfect for Bev and Amy. Though they might not realize it, they had brought joy into his life, and they deserved to have a special Christmas.

Satisfied that everything was finally ready, Dan put the potatoes in a kettle of cold water, grabbed his coat and gloves, and headed out the door. It was time to pick up his dinner guests.

A short time later, he stood in front of Bev's door, glad she hadn't refused his offer of a ride. It would have been difficult for her and Amy to catch the bus, what with the child's ankle still slightly swollen, not to mention the weather, which had recently deepened the snow on the ground.

When Bev opened the door and smiled at Dan, it nearly took his breath away. She wore a lilac-colored gown with a wide neckline and a skirt that dropped just below her knees. And this time she had on a pair of hose. "You're beautiful," he murmured.

"Thanks. You look pretty handsome yourself."

He glanced at his navy-blue slacks and matching blazer. Nothing out of the ordinary, but if she thought he looked handsome, that was all right by him.

Bev opened the door wider. "Come in and I'll get our coats."

Dan stepped into the living room and spotted Amy sitting on the sofa, dressed in a frilly pink dress that matched her flushed cheeks.

"Hey, cutie. Ready to go?"

She nodded and grinned up at him. "I can't wait to give you my present, Uncle Dan."

He leaned over and scooped the child into his arms. "And I can't wait to receive it."

"That was a delicious meal," Bev said, amazed at how well Dan could cook. She was also surprised at the change that had come over him since Amy's accident. He'd driven Bev to the hospital and stayed with her until they knew Amy was okay. He had taken her home, back to the hospital the next day, and given them a ride to their apartment when Amy was released. Now, as they sat in Dan's living room inside his cozy brick home on the north end of town, Bev could honestly say she felt joy celebrating this Christmas.

"I'm glad you enjoyed dinner and equally glad I didn't burn anything." Dan nodded at Amy, who sat on the floor in front of the crackling fire he'd built earlier. "How about it, little one? Are you ready to open your presents?"

Amy scooted closer to the Christmas tree. "Yes!"

"Okay then. Who wants the first gift?"

"Me! Me!"

Dan chuckled and handed Amy a box. "I believe this one's from your mother."

Amy looked at Bev, and she nodded. "Go ahead and open it."

The child quickly tore off the wrapping, and when she lifted the lid and removed a delicate bisque doll, she squealed with delight. "She's beautiful, Mommy! Thank you!"

"You're welcome, sweetheart."

Amy smiled at Dan. "Can I give Mommy her present from me now?"

"Sure." Dan pointed to a small package wrapped in red paper. "It's that one."

Amy handed the gift to her mother and leaned against Dan's knee as Bev opened it.

"This is wonderful!" Bev exclaimed, as she held up a framed picture of Amy sitting on the patchwork quilt Dan's late wife had made. "How did you do this without me knowing?"

"When you were busy with customers, I took Amy into my photography studio and snapped her picture," Dan answered. "We bought the frame the day I took her Christmas shopping."

Bev kissed Amy's cheek and was tempted to do the same to Dan, but she caught herself in time. "Thank you both. I appreciate the picture and will find the right place to hang it when we go home."

"Here's my gift to you, Amy." Dan placed a large box in front of the child and helped her undo the flaps. Inside was a quilt—the same quilt that used to hang in Twice Loved and he'd used as a background for Amy's portrait.

Amy lifted the colorful covering and buried her face in it. "I love it, Uncle Dan. Thank you."

"It's a precious gift, Dan," Bev said, "but don't you think you should give the quilt to a family member?"

Dan took Bev's hand. "That's what I have in mind, all right."

Bev's heartbeat picked up speed. What exactly was he saying?

Dan reached into his jacket pocket and pulled out a flat green velvet box. He handed it to Bev with a smile.

She lifted the lid and gasped at the lovely gold locket inside. "It's beautiful. Thank you, Dan."

"Open the locket," he prompted.

She did—and soon discovered there was a picture of Amy on one side and a picture of Dan on the other.

"I'm in love with you, Bev," Dan said, as he leaned over and kissed her.

Bev's eyes filled with tears, and at first she could only nod in reply. When she finally found her voice, she whispered, "I love you, too."

Amy grinned from ear to ear, then handed Dan a large gift wrapped in green paper. "Here, Uncle Dan. This is for you, from me and Mommy."

Dan tore open the wrapping and lifted a brown teddy bear from the box. It had new eyes, patched paws, a pretty blue ribbon around its neck, and a sign on the front of its stomach that read: I am Twice Loved.

He tipped his head in question, and Bev smiled in response. "It was Amy's idea."

Dan gave Amy a hug, then lifted Bev's chin with his thumb. He kissed her once more and murmured, "I believe God brought the three of us together, and just like this bear and the quilt I gave Amy, we have been twice loved."

Other Books by Wanda E. Brunstetter:

Kentucky Brothers Series
The Journey

Indiana Cousins Series
A Cousin's Promise
A Cousin's Prayer
A Cousin's Challenge

Brides of Lehigh Canal Series
Kelly's Chance
Betsy's Return
Sarah's Choice

Daughters of Lancaster County Series
The Storekeeper's Daughter
The Quilter's Daughter
The Bishop's Daughter

Brides of Lancaster County Series
A Merry Heart
Looking for a Miracle
Plain and Fancy
The Hope Chest

Sisters of Holmes County Series
A Sister's Secret
A Sister's Test
A Sister's Hope

Brides of Webster County Series
Going Home
On Her Own
Dear to Me
Allison's Journey

White Christmas Pie
Lydia's Charm

Nonfiction
The Simple Life
A Celebration of the Simple Life
Wanda E. Brunstetter's Amish Friends Cookbook
Wanda E. Brunstetter's Amish Friends Cookbook, Vol. 2
Wanda E. Brunstetter's Amish Friends Cookbook: Desserts

Children's Books
Rachel Yoder—Always Trouble Somewhere Series (8 books)
The Wisdom of Solomon

About the Author

Wanda E. Brunstetter is a bestselling author who enjoys writing Amish-themed, as well as historical novels. Descended from Anabaptists herself, Wanda became deeply interested in the Plain People when she married her husband, Richard who grew up in a Mennonite church in Pennsylvania. Wanda and her husband live in Washington State, but take every opportunity to visit their Amish friends in various communities across the country, gathering further information about the Amish way of life.

Wanda and her husband have two grown children and six grandchildren. In her spare time, Wanda enjoys photography, ventriloquism, gardening, reading, stamping, and having fun with her family.

In addition to her novels, Wanda has written Amish cookbooks, Amish devotionals, several Amish children's books, as well as numerous novellas, stories, articles, poems, and puppet scripts.

Visit Wanda's Web site at www.wandabrunstetter.com and feel free to e-mail her at wanda@wandabrunstetter.com.

If you enjoyed

also read

Three stories of light-hearted romance from bestselling author Wanda E. Brunstetter prove *Love Finds a Way*. Widow Lorna Patterson returns to college looking for education not romance. Then she meets fellow student and culinary novice Evan Bailey. Will his persistence have her re-thinking love? When Shelia Nickels searches for her grandmother's doll her hunt leads to antique dealer Dwaine Woods's door. But will she find love instead of a lost treasure? Wendy Campbell doesn't want a relationship, but her father does. . .for her. Will his matchmaking end with an unexpected romance for Wendy and paramedic Kyle Rogers?

Available January 2012